THE INHERITANCE

THE HARRY STARKE NOVELS
BOOK 25

BLAIR HOWARD

For Ryder, my beautiful granddaughter

Printed Cleveland, TN, USA
Print Paperback ISBN: 979-8-9988024-3-0
Blair Howard Books
BlairHoward@BlairHowardBooks.com

1

THE DAUGHTER

THE WOMAN SITTING ACROSS FROM MY DESK LOOKED like she hadn't slept in a week. Lisa Brennan was probably in her early forties, well-dressed in that understated way that usually means money, but her hands shook as she reached for the coffee cup Margo, Heather's PA, had brought her. Dark circles shadowed her eyes, and she kept glancing toward the door like she expected someone to walk in and drag her away.

The morning light filtering through my office windows cast harsh shadows across her face, emphasizing the stress lines that seemed too deep for someone her age. Her designer handbag sat clutched in her lap like a shield, and I noticed she'd been picking at her cuticles until they bled. The nervous energy radiating from her was almost palpable, filling my office with the kind of tension that made even seasoned investigators like me pay attention.

I'd seen that look before. Fear mixed with desperation, the kind that comes when someone you love is in danger and nobody will listen to you. It was the same expression I'd seen on Amanda's face when she thought I was taking too many risks, the same look Kate got when a case started going sideways. This woman was genuinely terrified.

Her clothing told a story too—expensive but slightly wrinkled, as if she'd been wearing the same outfit for days. The silk blouse that probably cost more than most people's weekly salary was creased from constant fidgeting, and her jewelry, while tasteful and costly, seemed to weigh her down rather than complement her appearance. Everything about Lisa Brennan suggested wealth in crisis, privilege under siege.

"Ms. Brennan," I said, settling back in my chair, "why don't you start from the beginning? Tell me what's got you so worried."

She took a sip of coffee, grimaced slightly, then set the cup down with trembling fingers. The simple act seemed to take considerable effort, as if she were forcing herself to go through the motions of normalcy when nothing about her situation was normal.

"It's my father, Mr. Starke. Walter Brennan. I think someone is trying to kill him."

I'd heard that line more times than I could count over the years, and ninety percent of the time it turned out to be paranoia, family drama, or someone looking for attention. But something in Lisa Brennan's voice made me pay attention. This wasn't hysteria or attention-seeking. This was genuine fear, the kind that comes from watching someone you care about slip away and feeling powerless to stop it.

"What makes you think that?" I asked, keeping my tone neutral. I'd learned long ago not to dismiss these concerns too quickly, even when they seemed far-fetched. Sometimes the most outlandish stories turned out to be true.

"Three weeks ago, my father changed his will." She reached into her purse and pulled out a tissue, dabbing at her eyes. Her hands were still shaking. "He cut me and my brother Mark out completely. He hasn't signed it yet... at least I don't think he has. But everything—his entire estate—goes to his caregiver, Maya Santos."

I made a note on my legal pad. Will changes weren't uncommon, especially with elderly clients who'd become isolated from their families. But the timing was worth noting.

"That's not necessarily suspicious, Ms. Brennan," I said. "People change their wills for all sorts of reasons. Sometimes they feel their children don't need the money, or they want to reward someone who's been particularly helpful to them."

"But that's not all." Her voice dropped to almost a whisper, and she leaned forward in her chair. "Yesterday, he called me, terrified. He said someone has been poisoning him... slowly. He's been saving food samples, pills, anything he thinks might be contaminated. He's got them stored in little containers in his bedroom, labeled with dates and times."

Now that was interesting. Paranoid behavior could be a sign of mental decline, but it could also be a rational response to a real threat. The fact that he was documenting everything suggested he was still thinking clearly, at least on some level.

"He said he's been feeling weak, dizzy, sometimes nauseous after meals. But when I suggested calling the police or taking him to the hospital, he got agitated and said Maya told him he was having paranoid delusions. She convinced him that if he made these accusations, people would think he was losing his mind."

I set down my pen and studied Lisa's face. "Has your father shown signs of mental decline recently?"

Lisa's face crumpled, and for a moment I thought she might break down completely. "That's what everyone keeps asking me. Yes, he's seventy-eight. Yes, he's been more forgetful lately, more suspicious of people, more isolated. But Mr. Starke, my father built a construction empire from nothing. He started with a single truck and a handful of tools, and by the time he retired, Brennan Construction was one of the biggest general contractors in the Southeast."

She wiped her eyes and continued, "He's always been sharp, always been careful about details. Even now, when he talks about business, about investments, about his properties, he's completely lucid. If he says someone is poisoning him, if he's documenting symptoms and saving evidence…"

She trailed off, but I could fill in the blanks. "You believe him."

"I have to. He's all the family I have left, really. My mother died eight years ago, and Mark and I, we haven't been close to Dad in years. We had our differences about his business practices, about money, about a lot of things. But the thought that someone might be taking advantage of him, might be killing him..." She wiped her eyes again. "I can't just sit by and do nothing."

I leaned back in my chair, processing what she'd told me. Elder abuse was more common than most people wanted to admit, and financial exploitation was often the first step in a larger pattern of abuse. Caregivers who isolated their victims from family were frequently the perpetrators, gradually gaining control over every aspect of their client's life.

"Tell me about Maya Santos," I said.

"She's been Dad's home health aide for about six months. She's young, maybe mid-thirties, very attractive. Latina, I think, though she speaks perfect English without an accent. She came with excellent references from an agency in Atlanta, and at first I was grateful someone was looking after him."

Lisa shifted in her chair, her expression growing more troubled. "Dad had been resistant to having help in the house. He's always been independent, proud, stubborn as hell. But after Mom died, he started declining. Not mentally, but physically. He had a nasty fall about a year ago, broke his wrist, and after that he seemed frailer somehow."

"So you and your brother arranged for the caregiver?" I asked.

"Actually, no. Maya just showed up one day, said the agency had received a call requesting services. Dad claimed he'd called them himself, though he'd never mentioned it to Mark or me. But she was so professional, so caring, that we didn't question it. Maybe we should have."

That was the first real red flag. Legitimate caregivers didn't just show up unannounced, and reputable agencies always confirmed arrangements with family members. If Maya Santos had initiated contact with Walter Brennan, that suggested a level of premeditation that made everything else more suspicious.

"What happened after she started working for your father?" I asked.

"At first, everything seemed fine. She was there during the day, helping with meals, medication reminders, light housekeeping. Dad seemed happier, more energetic. But gradually, she started limiting our visits. She'd say Dad needed rest, that we were upsetting him, that our arguments about his business decisions were causing him stress."

Lisa's voice turned bitter. "Then Dad started canceling our weekly lunches, saying Maya thought they were too much for him. When I called to check on him, she'd answer the phone and say he was sleeping, or having a bad day, or couldn't come to the phone. Pretty soon, I was lucky if I talked to him once a week."

"And now she's the sole beneficiary of his will." I said.

"Eighty million dollars, Mr. Starke. Dad's entire fortune, including the house, his investments, his land holdings, everything. Maya claims she's just following doctor's orders, trying to keep Dad calm and healthy. But if someone wanted to isolate an elderly man from his family, what better way than to convince him his children are the source of his problems?"

I made another note, this time underlining it. Eighty million was enough to kill for, especially for someone who'd positioned herself as the victim's only friend and protector. If Maya Santos was running a long con, she'd set it up perfectly.

"Who else has access to your father's house?" I asked.

"There's a cook, Helen Foster, who's been with the family for fifteen years. She comes in five days a week and usually leaves around two in the afternoon. James Morrison is the groundskeeper—he's worked for Dad for twenty years. He lives in a small apartment above the garage. And Ruth Webb comes in twice a week to clean, Mondays and Thursdays. That's it, as far as I know."

"What about your brother?" I asked. "Where does he stand on all this?"

Lisa's expression darkened, and she looked down at her hands. "Mark thinks I'm being paranoid. He says Dad always favored his employees over his children anyway, so why should this be different? He thinks Maya is probably a nice woman who's genuinely caring for Dad, and that I'm just upset about losing my inheritance."

She looked up at me, and I could see the hurt in her eyes. "But Mark has his own problems. His restaurant failed last year—he lost everything, including his house. I know he's been hoping for his inheritance to bail him out of debt. He's borrowed money from some pretty dangerous people, Mr. Starke. The kind who don't just write off bad loans."

Interesting. I thought. *So both siblings had financial motives if their father died with the original will in place. But if Maya Santos inherited everything, they'd get nothing. Unless they could prove she'd manipulated or harmed the old man, in which case the will might be contested successfully.*

"Ms. Brennan, I have to ask—what's your financial situation?"

She flushed, clearly embarrassed. "Not great, to be honest. I own an art gallery downtown, Brennan Fine Arts. It's been in the family for twenty years, but the market has been tough lately. I'm behind on rent, behind on my business loan payments. I've been hoping Dad might help me modernize, expand the space, maybe move to a better location. But if Maya gets everything..." She shrugged helplessly.

So both children needed money, but neither would benefit from their father's death under the current will. That actually made Lisa's story more credible. If she were planning to kill her father for his money, she wouldn't have let him change the will first. Unless she was planning to contest it, but that would be a risky strategy with no guarantee of success.

"Have you spoken to the police about your father's concerns?" I asked.

"No," she replied. "Dad was adamant that I not involve them. He said Maya convinced him that if the police got involved, they might declare him mentally incompetent and put him in a facility. He's terrified of losing his independence, of being forced to leave his home."

It was a classic manipulation tactic. Isolate the victim, make them dependent on you, then make them afraid of outside help. It was looking more and more like Maya Santos had run this playbook before.

"Mister Starke," Lisa said, leaning forward in her chair, "I know how this sounds. Greedy children trying to protect their inheritance, maybe even planning something terrible themselves. But I swear to you, this isn't about the money. If Dad wants to leave everything to charity, fine. If he wants to give it all to Maya because she's genuinely caring for him, I can live with that."

Her voice broke slightly. "But if someone is taking advantage of him, maybe even killing him slowly while pretending to care for him... I can't live with doing nothing. I can't live with the thought that I stood by and let it happen because I was afraid of looking like a greedy daughter."

I believed her. There was something in her voice, her body language, the way she'd presented the facts without trying to oversell her case, that convinced me she was telling the truth. At least as she saw it. Whether her perception matched reality remained to be seen, but her fear was genuine.

"My daily rate is five hundred plus expenses," I said. "If this turns into a long investigation, it could get expensive. Elder abuse cases can be complex, time-consuming, and require a lot of surveillance and docu-mentation."

"I don't care about the cost. I'll mortgage the gallery if I have to. I just want to know if my father is safe, if someone is really trying to hurt him, or if I'm losing my mind along with him."

I pulled out a contract and slid it across the desk. "Jacque will help you with that."

She picked it up, glanced at it, put it down again, then looked up at me and nodded.

"I'll need to meet with your father," I said. "I'd like to observe the household dynamics, and talk to the staff if possible. If Maya Santos is legitimate, that should quickly become clear. If she's running some kind of con, or if she's actually harming your father…"

"You'll expose her?" she asked.

"I'll get you the truth, Ms. Brennan. Whatever that turns out to be. But I have to warn you, sometimes the truth isn't what people want to hear. If your father is genuinely declining mentally, if Maya Santos is a legitimate caregiver doing her job, you'll have to accept that."

She reached out, picked up my pen and signed the contract without even reading it, which told me how desperate she was. People who sign legal documents without reading them are either very trusting, very stupid or very frightened. Given everything else she'd told me, I was betting on frightened.

"When can you start?" she asked.

"This afternoon. I'll need your father's address and a way to contact him directly. Do you have a key to the house, or should I just show up at the front door?"

She wrote the information on the back of a business

card. "He's usually alone with Maya in the afternoons. Helen, the cook, leaves around two, and Ruth only comes in Mondays and Thursdays. If you're going to see him, sometime before Helen leaves might be the best time to get a sense of the household dynamics."

"And you're sure Maya will be there?"

"She's always there. She lives in the house now. She says Dad needs round-the-clock care. That's another thing that happened gradually. First she was just coming during the day, then she started staying late when he had a bad spell, and then staying overnight when he had trouble sleeping. Now she has her own room and acts like she owns the place."

I stood up and extended my hand. "I'll drive out there this afternoon and introduce myself. Try not to worry, Ms. Brennan. If someone's taking advantage of your father, we'll find out. If he's genuinely declining and Maya is providing proper care, we'll find that out too."

She shook my hand gratefully, holding on perhaps a moment longer than necessary. "Thank you, Mr. Starke. I know Dad can be difficult, suspicious of strangers, set in his ways. But if you can just observe what's happening in that house, if you can talk to him when Maya isn't hovering over him…"

"I'll be in touch within twenty-four hours," I said. "One way or another, we'll get to the bottom of it."

After she left, I sat back in my chair and stared at the contract. Elder abuse cases were always tricky because the line between legitimate care and manipulation could be razor thin. Caregivers who isolated their clients from family often claimed they were protecting vulnerable people from relatives who only showed up when they wanted money. Sometimes that was true. Sometimes families were more interested in preserving their inheritance than in protecting their elderly relatives.

But eighty million dollars was a powerful motive for murder. And if Maya Santos had convinced Walter Brennan to change his will, and then convinced him his paranoid fears about poisoning were just delusions, she had the perfect setup. The old man could die of "natural causes" brought on by stress and age, and no one would question the devoted caregiver who'd tried so hard to keep him healthy and comfortable.

I picked up the phone and dialed TJ's extension. "You busy this afternoon?"

"Nothing that can't wait," he replied. "What's up, Harry?"

"Feel like visiting a mansion? We might have ourselves a genuine mystery for once."

"About damn time," he replied. "These insurance fraud cases are starting to bore me to death. What kind of mystery?"

"Possible elder abuse, financial exploitation, maybe even attempted murder. A rich old man, a suspicious caregiver, desperate family members, and eighty million reasons for someone to commit murder."

There was a pause, then TJ chuckled. "Now that sounds more like it. What's the plan?"

"Meet me in the parking lot at one," I said. "And TJ? Bring your camera and that little recording device you're so fond of. Something tells me we're going to need to document everything we see and hear."

"You got it, boss. Should I bring anything else? Lock picks, listening devices, body armor?"

I smiled. TJ always enjoyed the more dramatic aspects of our work, probably a holdover from his military days. "Just your eyes and ears for now. If this turns into something more complicated, we'll adjust accordingly."

I hung up and looked at the address Lisa Brennan had given me. Signal Mountain Acres was one of the most exclusive areas in Chattanooga. Whatever Walter Brennan had built his fortune on, it had served him well. The question was whether Maya Santos was planning to help herself to it.

One way or another, I was going to find out.

2

THE MANSION

THE BRENNAN ESTATE SAT ON THREE ACRES OF perfectly manicured grounds at the end of a winding drive that screamed old money and good taste. The house itself was a sprawling Tudor revival, probably built in the nineteen-twenties when Chattanooga's industrial boom made millionaires out of men who knew how to move dirt and pour concrete. Ivy climbed the brick walls in carefully controlled patterns, and the slate roof looked like it had been cleaned yesterday.

The approach to the mansion was designed to impress, with ancient oak trees forming a natural canopy over the drive and carefully maintained landscaping that spoke of both wealth and attention to detail. The grounds showed the kind of meticulous care that required professional maintenance: every hedge trimmed to perfection and every flower bed arranged with artistic precision.

TJ whistled as we pulled in through the wrought-iron gates. "Nice digs. Remind me to get into the construction business in my next life."

"Little late for that career change," I said as I parked the Range Rover next to a pristine Mercedes sedan that probably cost more than most people's houses. "But I'll keep it in mind for my retirement planning."

The front door was solid oak, with stained glass panels depicting some kind of family crest. I pressed the doorbell and heard chimes echoing through what sounded like a very large house. After a moment, footsteps approached, and the door opened to reveal a woman who had to be Maya Santos.

Lisa Brennan's description hadn't done her justice. Maya was strikingly beautiful in that effortless way that comes from good genes and careful maintenance. She appeared to be in her mid-thirties, as Lisa had said, dark hair pulled back in a professional-looking bun and intelligent brown eyes that seemed to take in everything at once. She wore scrubs, but they were the expensive kind that actually fit properly, and her jewelry was understated but real.

"Can I help you?" she asked, her voice warm but cautious. There was no trace of an accent, just educated American English with maybe a hint of the South.

"Ms. Santos? I'm Harry Starke, and this is my associate TJ Bron. Lisa Brennan hired us to check on her father's welfare. She's concerned."

Maya's expression didn't change, but I caught a slight tightening around her eyes. "I see. And what exactly is Ms. Brennan concerned about?"

"Why don't we discuss that with Mr. Brennan? Is he available?"

She hesitated for just a moment too long. "He's having a difficult day. The stress of family conflicts has been hard on him lately. Perhaps it would be better if you came back another time."

"I understand he's been worried about his health," I said. "We'd like to hear his concerns directly, if that's possible."

Maya glanced over her shoulder, then stepped reluctantly aside. "Very well. But please keep in mind that Mr. Brennan is elderly and fragile. Any agitation could be harmful to his condition."

She led us through a foyer that belonged in a museum, past a living room that looked like it had been decorated by someone with unlimited funds and conservative taste. The furniture was expensive but comfortable, the kind of pieces that lasted for generations. Family portraits lined the walls, including several that showed a younger Walter Brennan in various business settings, always looking confident and in control.

The interior of the mansion reflected the same attention to detail as the exterior, with custom millwork, expensive fabrics, and artwork that suggested both wealth and genuine appreciation for quality. Everything was perfectly maintained, creating an atmosphere of timeless elegance and substantial prosperity.

"He's in the library," Maya said, knocking gently on a set of double doors before opening them. "Mr. Brennan? You have visitors."

The library was everything you'd expect of a successful businessman's home office. Floor-to-ceiling bookshelves lined three walls, filled with leather-bound volumes that looked as if they'd actually been read. A massive mahogany desk dominated one corner, and comfortable leather chairs were arranged around a fireplace that could have roasted a small pig.

Walter Brennan sat in a wingback chair near the windows, and it was immediately clear why his daughter was worried. The man in the photographs had been robust, commanding, the kind of person who filled a room with his presence. The man looking up at us now seemed to have shrunk inside his clothes. He was still tall, probably six-foot-two in his prime, but his frame had the fragile quality that comes with age and illness. His hair was white and thin, his face deeply lined, and his pale blue eyes had a watery quality that suggested either illness or medication.

But when he looked at us, those eyes were sharp and suspicious. Whatever was happening to Walter Brennan physically, his mind appeared to be alert.

"Who are you?" he asked, his voice stronger than his appearance suggested. "Maya, I told you I didn't want to see anyone today."

"Mr. Brennan, my name is Harry Starke. I'm a private investigator. Your daughter Lisa asked me to come see you."

His expression shifted, surprise mixing with what looked like relief. "Lisa sent you? Is she all right? I haven't heard from her in days."

Maya stepped forward. "Mr. Brennan, you spoke

with Lisa yesterday. Remember? She called during your afternoon rest period, and you said you were too tired to talk long."

Walter frowned, and, for a moment, he looked confused. "Did I? I don't... yesterday is a bit fuzzy. I haven't been sleeping well."

The confusion could have been natural forgetfulness, or the result of medication, but the timing was suspicious. If Maya was controlling Walter's contact with his family, she would certainly want to minimize any memory of those conversations.

"That's why we're here," I said, taking a seat in the chair across from him. TJ remained standing, positioning himself where he could observe both Walter and Maya. "Lisa is concerned about your health. She said you've been feeling unwell."

Walter's eyes brightened, and he leaned forward in his chair. "Finally, someone who'll listen, he said. "Maya thinks I'm losing my mind, but I know what's happening to me. Someone is trying to poison me."

"Mr. Brennan," Maya said gently, "we've discussed this. Your symptoms are consistent with normal aging and the stress you've been under."

"Normal aging?" Walter's voice rose slightly. "Maya's been very good to me, but lately I can't shake the feeling that something's wrong."

He turned to me, his eyes had an urgent look about them. "I've been saving samples. Food, pills, everything. I label them with dates and times. I keep them in containers in my bedroom. I know it sounds crazy, but someone is doing this to me. The weakness, the dizziness, the nausea. It's not natural."

Maya's expression remained patient, but I caught a flash of something that might have been annoyance. "Mr. Brennan has been experiencing some paranoid episodes lately. It's not uncommon in elderly patients, especially those dealing with isolation and family stress."

"I'm not paranoid," Walter said, his voice growing stronger. "I built a company from nothing. I employed hundreds of people, managed millions of dollars in projects. I know the difference between paranoia and reality."

The exchange revealed an important dynamic. Walter was clearly struggling with confusion and memory problems, but when he focused on his concerns about being poisoned, his thinking seemed remarkably clear and organized.

"Of course you do," I said. "Can you show me these samples you've been collecting?"

Walter started to stand, but Maya moved quickly to his side. "I don't think that's a good idea. He needs to rest, and this kind of agitation isn't healthy for him."

"I can decide what's healthy for me," Walter snapped, more forcefully than I'd expected. "This is still my house, and I'm still capable of making my own decisions."

The exchange was telling. Maya's concern seemed genuine, but there was something controlling about the way she tried to manage every aspect of Walter's interactions. It could be a protective instinct, or it could be something else entirely.

"Mr. Brennan," I said, "why don't you tell me when you first started feeling unwell?"

He settled back in his chair, clearly grateful for someone who was willing to listen. "About two months ago, I started having episodes. Dizzy spells, nausea, weakness in my legs. At first I thought it was just getting old, but then I noticed the pattern."

"What kind of pattern?" I asked.

"It happened after meals sometimes," he replied, "or after taking my medications. Not every time, but often enough that I started paying attention. And the symptoms were always the same: weakness, dizziness, sometimes a burning sensation in my stomach."

Maya interrupted. "Mr. Brennan, Dr. Walker explained those symptoms could be caused by a dozen different things. Your blood pressure medication can cause dizziness, and your age makes you more sensitive to changes in routine."

"Then why don't I feel sick when I eat food I prepare myself?" Walter asked. "Why do the symptoms only happen when Maya is here?"

That was a significant accusation, and Maya's reaction was telling. She didn't get defensive or angry, which might have been the natural response if she were innocent. Instead, she looked sad, almost disappointed.

"Mr. Brennan," she said, gently. "I'm here every day. If you only feel sick when I'm here, it's because I'm always here. Correlation isn't causation."

It was a reasonable explanation, but Walter wasn't

buying it. "Then explain why I feel better when I skip meals. Explain why I've lost fifteen pounds in two months, despite eating regularly."

I looked at Maya. "Has Mr. Brennan seen a doctor about the weight loss?"

"Of course. Dr. Walker has run comprehensive tests. Blood work, urinalysis, even a CT scan. Everything came back normal for a man his age."

"What about testing for toxins?" I asked. "Heavy metals, plant alkaloids, anything like that?"

Maya hesitated. "Doctor Walker didn't feel that was necessary. Mr. Brennan's symptoms are consistent with stress and normal aging."

Walter leaned forward again. "That's what I keep telling everyone. If they're so sure I'm fine, why won't they test for poisons? What are they afraid of finding?"

It was a good question. If Walter was suffering from paranoid delusions, comprehensive testing would prove that and put his mind at ease. If he was actually being poisoned, the tests would reveal it. The fact that his doctor hadn't ordered toxicology screens suggested either incompetence or complicity.

"Mr. Brennan," I said, "can you show me where you keep these samples?"

He started to rise again, but this time Maya didn't try to stop him. "They're in my bedroom. I'll show you."

We followed him through the house, and I was struck by how well he moved once he got going. His step was uncertain at first, but he seemed to gain strength as we walked. Either he was having a good moment, or the weakness he'd described was episodic rather than constant.

His bedroom was on the second floor, a spacious suite with windows overlooking the back gardens. The furniture was antique but well-maintained, and everything was meticulously organized. Walter led us to a dresser near the windows and opened the top drawer.

Inside were dozens of small containers—pill bottles, baby food jars, small Tupperware containers—each labeled with dates and descriptions in Walter's careful handwriting. "Dinner soup, Tuesday, March 15th." "Morning pills, Thursday, March 18th." "Afternoon tea, Sunday, March 21st."

"I save a sample whenever I feel sick afterward," Walter explained. "I know it's not much, but maybe it's enough for testing."

I picked up one of the containers and examined the label. The handwriting was shaky but legible, and the dates went back almost two months. If Walter was suffering from dementia or paranoid delusions, this level of organization and consistency seemed unlikely.

"Have you had any of these tested?" I asked.

"I tried to take some to a lab, but they said I needed a doctor's order. When I asked Dr. Walker, she said it wasn't necessary and that I should throw them away."

TJ stepped closer to examine the collection. "That's a lot of samples," he said, thoughtfully. "And very well organized."

"I was a project manager for forty years," Walter said with a trace of his former pride. "I know how to document things properly."

Maya watched from the doorway, her expression unreadable. "Mr. Brennan, this obsession with poison isn't healthy. You're making yourself sick with worry."

"I'm making myself sick?" Walter's voice rose. "I'm not the one putting things in my food. I'm not the one who shows up every time I try to call my children. I'm not the one who changed my will."

"You changed your will because you wanted to," Maya said firmly. "I never asked you to do that. I never even suggested it."

The argument was getting heated, and I could see Walter becoming more agitated. His hands were shaking, and his face was flushed. Whatever was happening between him and Maya, the stress was clearly affecting his health.

"Mr. Brennan," I said, "why don't you sit down for a moment? This is a lot to process."

He looked at me gratefully and sank into a chair near the window. "I'm sorry. I get worked up when people don't believe me. Maya's been very good to me, but lately I can't shake the feeling that something's wrong."

"It's all right," I said. "Feeling confused and suspicious can be frightening. But that's why we're here; to figure out what's really happening."

Maya stepped into the room. "Mr. Brennan, you should rest now. All this excitement isn't good for you."

"I'm fine," Walter said, but his voice was weaker now. "I just need people to listen to me."

I looked around the room, taking in the details. Everything was neat and organized, from the carefully labeled samples to the precisely arranged furniture. This didn't look like the room of someone suffering from serious mental decline.

"Mr. Brennan, who else has access to your food and medications?"

"Helen prepares most of my meals. She's been with us for fifteen years, since before my wife died. James takes care of the grounds, but he doesn't come inside much. Ruth cleans twice a week. And Maya, of course. She's here all the time now."

"What about your children? Do they visit often?"

Walter's expression darkened. "Not as much as they used to. Maya says they upset me, that I'm healthier when I don't have to deal with family drama. She's probably right. Lisa and Mark only seem to call when they want something."

"That's not true," Maya said quietly. "They call regularly. You just don't always remember the conversations."

Walter looked confused again. "Do they? I… sometimes the days run together. Maybe I'm not remembering right."

The confusion seemed genuine, and it was troubling. Either Walter was experiencing some form of cognitive decline, or something was affecting his memory and perception. If he was being drugged, that could explain both the physical symptoms and the mental confusion.

"Mr. Brennan," I said, "would you be willing to have some of these samples tested independently? Not through your regular doctor, but through a private lab?"

His eyes brightened. "You'd do that? You'd help me find out what's wrong?"

"If you want us to, yes. But I have to warn you, the results might not be what you expect. If the tests come back negative, if there's no evidence of poisoning, you'll need to accept that and work with your doctors to find other explanations for your symptoms."

Walter nodded eagerly. "I understand. I just want to know the truth."

Maya stepped forward. "Mr. Brennan, I think this is a mistake. You're going to spend money on unnecessary tests, and when they come back normal, you'll just find some other explanation for your symptoms. This obsession is consuming your life."

"It's my money and my life," Walter snapped with surprising firmness. "And if I want to spend it finding out why I feel like I'm dying, that's my choice."

The exchange revealed a lot about the household dynamics. Walter seemed genuinely convinced he was being poisoned, while Maya appeared to be trying to manage his emotional state rather than address his specific accusations. Either Walter was suffering from elaborate paranoid delusions.

"All right," I said. "I'll arrange for some of these samples to be tested. In the meantime, I'd like to talk to the other people who work here. Helen, James, and Ruth."

"Helen should be in the kitchen," Walter said. "She usually stays until two to prepare dinner. James is probably in the greenhouse. He's been working on the spring plantings. And Ruth will be here tomorrow."

Maya looked uncomfortable. "I'm not sure that's necessary. The staff are very loyal, very professional. I don't think they'd appreciate being interrogated."

"Not interrogated," I said. "Just a friendly conversation. If there's nothing to hide, there's nothing to worry about."

"Of course," Maya said, but her tone suggested otherwise. "I'll show you to the kitchen."

As we left Walter's room, I caught TJ's eye. He nodded slightly, indicating he'd observed the same things I had. Walter Brennan might be elderly and confused, but he wasn't crazy. His concerns were specific, documented, and consistent. Whether they were based in reality remained to be seen, but they deserved to be taken seriously.

The kitchen was at the back of the house, a large, modern space that had probably been renovated recently. A woman in her sixties was working at the stove, stirring something that smelled like chicken soup. She looked up as we entered.

"Helen," Maya said, "these are the investigators Lisa hired. They'd like to ask you some questions."

Helen Foster wiped her hands on her apron and nodded politely. "I figured someone would show up, eventually. Lisa's been worried sick about her father."

"What do you think about Mr. Brennan's concerns?" I asked.

Helen glanced at Maya, then back at me. "I think he's a scared old man who doesn't understand what's happening to his body. But I've been cooking for this family for fifteen years, and I've never put anything in their food that shouldn't be there."

"Has he been eating normally?" I asked.

"His appetite's been poor lately," she replied. "He picks at his food, claims it tastes funny. But his taste buds are probably changing. That happens with age."

"What about his medications? Do you help with those?"

"That's Maya's department. I just cook the meals and keep the kitchen clean."

Maya stepped forward. "Mr. Brennan has several medications for blood pressure, cholesterol, and sleep. I help him remember to take them on schedule."

"Who prescribes them?" I asked.

"Doctor Walker, his primary care physician," she replied. "She's been treating him for several years."

I made a mental note to follow up with Dr. Walker. If Walter was being poisoned, his medications would be the most likely delivery method. They were taken regularly, prepared by someone else, and any changes in effectiveness could be attributed to normal variations in absorption or metabolism.

"Helen," I said, "have you noticed any changes in Mr. Brennan's behavior lately?"

She hesitated, glancing again at Maya. "He's been more suspicious, more worried about things. But that's understandable given his age and his health problems."

"What about his relationship with his children?" I asked.

"That's not my place to say," Helen replied firmly. "This family's business is their own."

Maya nodded approvingly. "Helen is very discreet. She understands the importance of privacy."

But I caught something in Helen's expression, a flicker of something that might have been concern or disagreement. She was holding back, probably out of loyalty to the family or fear of getting involved in something complicated.

"Well," I said, "we won't take up any more of your time, Helen. Thank you for talking with us."

As we left the kitchen, Maya led us back toward the front door, saying, "I hope you can see that Mr. Brennan is well cared for. His concerns are understandable, but unfounded."

"We'll know more after the test results come back," I said. "In the meantime, we may need to come back and talk to him again."

"Of course. But please remember, he's fragile. Too much excitement or stress could be harmful."

We stepped outside, and I turned back to face her. "Ms. Santos, how long have you been working as a caregiver?"

"About five years. I have a nursing degree and specialized training in geriatric care."

"And before that?"

"I worked in hospitals, mostly in Atlanta. I prefer private care. It allows me to develop real relationships with my clients."

"Have any of your previous clients made similar accusations?"

Her expression hardened slightly. "Elderly people sometimes become suspicious of their caregivers. It's a known phenomenon in geriatric psychology. They feel vulnerable and look for someone to blame for their declining health."

It was a reasonable explanation, but something about her tone bothered me. She was too smooth, too prepared with answers to difficult questions. Either she'd dealt with this situation before, or she'd spent time thinking about how to respond to such accusations.

"Thank you for your time," I said. "We'll be in touch."

As we walked back to the car, TJ shook his head. "That woman is hiding something. I can't put my finger on it, but she's not telling us everything."

"I agree," I said. "The question is whether she's hiding something innocent or something deadly."

"What about the old man? You think he's really being poisoned?"

I thought about Walter's carefully labeled samples, his specific complaints, his obvious fear. "I have a feeling someone may be trying to kill him. The question is who."

3

FAMILY DYNAMICS

BACK AT THE OFFICE, I FOUND JACQUE HUNCHED OVER her computer, surrounded by printouts and legal documents. She looked up as I walked in; her reading glasses perched on the end of her nose in a way that made her look like a librarian who'd stumbled into detective work.

Jacque's kind of special to me. She's my PA and business partner. Jamaican by birth, she's thirty-five years old, but looks ten years younger. She's tall—five nine—a little skinny, has beautiful skin the color of coffee and cream, bushy black hair, and a captivating smile. She has a master's degree in business administration and a bachelor's in criminology, which is one of the reasons I hired her, even before she got out of college. The main reason being... well, I liked her. When she smiles, she lights up the room. She has an amazing sense of humor and a charming personality. She can be serious when she needs to be, the more so when she's around me, and in the office. She's assertive, self-assured, and smart. She runs the agency like a well-oiled machine. She's also fiercely protective of me, the company's reputation, my privacy, and my well-being. She's also gay.

The late afternoon sun slanted through the office windows, casting long shadows across the cluttered workspace where Jacque had been conducting her financial investigation. Her desk was covered with bank statements, property records, and legal documents that painted a detailed picture of the Brennan family's complex financial situation.

"How'd it go at the mansion?" she asked, pushing the glasses up her nose.

"Interesting. What have you found about the Brennan family finances?"

"More than you probably want to know." She gestured to the papers scattered across her desk. "Walter Brennan is worth exactly what his daughter told you—eighty point two million, to be precise. Most of it's tied up in real estate and conservative investments, but there's about two million in liquid assets."

I slouched down into the chair across from her desk and rested my cheek in my right hand, my elbow on the arm of the chair. "What about the kids?" I asked.

"That's where it gets complicated." Jacque pulled out a folder marked 'Lisa Brennan' and opened it. "Her art gallery is hemorrhaging money. She's three months behind on rent, owes forty thousand in back taxes to the IRS, and has a business loan that's about to go into default."

"How much does she owe total?"

"Conservative estimate? About two hundred thousand, not counting potential penalties and interest. Her personal finances aren't much better. She's leveraged her house, maxed out her credit cards, and borrowed against her life insurance."

I whistled low. "That's serious desperation money."

"It gets worse. Her brother Mark is in even deeper trouble." Jacque opened another folder. "His restaurant, Morrison's Bistro, closed six months ago owing suppliers, employees, and the landlord a combined total of three hundred and fifty thousand dollars."

"Ouch," I muttered.

"But that's not the worst of it. According to my sources, Mark borrowed money from some very unfriendly people to try to keep the restaurant afloat. Tommy Torrino's organization, specifically."

I sat up straighter. Tommy Torrino was a loan shark with connections to organized crime in Atlanta. People who couldn't pay back Tommy's loans had a tendency to end up in the hospital, or worse.

"How much does he owe Torrino?"

"One hundred thousand, plus interest that's been compounding for four months. At Tommy's rates, that's probably closer to one-fifty by now."

"Jesus. No wonder Lisa thought her brother might be desperate enough to kill for his inheritance."

The financial pressure on both siblings was staggering, creating powerful motives for wanting their father dead while his original will was still in effect. But the recent will change complicated the situation considerably, leaving both siblings with nothing to gain from

Walter's death unless they could prove Maya Santos had manipulated him.

"There's more," Jacque said, opening a third folder. "I did some digging into Maya Santos, and her story doesn't quite add up."

"What do you mean?"

"She claims to have a nursing degree from Emory, but when I called to verify, they said they had no record of a Maya Santos graduating from their program in the timeframe she specified."

That was interesting. "Could she have used a different name?" I said.

"Possible, but unlikely. I also checked her employment history with the agency that supposedly placed her with Walter Brennan. They confirmed they sent her, but when I asked for references from previous clients, they got very cagey. Said they couldn't release that information without a court order."

"Standard privacy policy, d'you think?" I asked. "Or are they hiding something?"

"Hard to say. But I did find something else. Maya Santos has worked for at least four other elderly clients in the past three years. All of them died while she was providing care."

Now that *was* interesting. I sat up and leaned forward. "Natural causes?"

Jacque nodded. "According to the death certificates, yes. Heart failure, stroke, complications from diabetes, and pneumonia. All believable for elderly people with health problems."

"But?" I asked.

"But all four of them changed their wills shortly before they died," she said, staring at me, "leaving substantial sums to Maya. Not everything, like Walter Brennan, but significant amounts. Fifty thousand here, a hundred thousand there."

Now that was a pattern. "Did any of the families contest the wills?"

"Two tried, but both settled out of court. Maya kept most of the money."

The pattern was deeply troubling and suggested that Walter Brennan wasn't Maya's first victim. If she had been systematically targeting vulnerable elderly people, she was far more dangerous than a simple opportunistic caregiver.

I sat back in my chair, processing the information. Four elderly clients, four deaths, four substantial inheritances. It could be coincidence; caregivers did develop close relationships with their clients, and grateful families sometimes left them money. But combined with Walter Brennan's specific fears about being poisoned, it suggested something much more sinister.

"Anything else?" I asked.

"One more thing. Maya's financial records show some interesting patterns. She's been living well above what a caregiver should be able to afford. She had a nice apartment—until she moved in with Walter—an expensive car, and she wears designer clothes. And she's made several large cash deposits over the past two years that don't correspond to her reported income."

"Inheritance money?"

"Probably. But here's the thing: she's also been making payments to someone or something that I can't track. Five thousand a month, always in cash, always on the same date. It's been going on for eighteen months."

"Blackmail?"

"Or paying off a partner. Or gambling debts. Could be anything, but it suggests she's got financial pressures of her own."

The mysterious monthly payments added another layer of complexity to Maya's situation. If she was being blackmailed or was part of a larger criminal organization, that would explain her systematic approach to targeting elderly victims.

I thought about Maya's composed demeanor, her smooth answers to difficult questions. She was definitely hiding something, but whether it was murder or just garden-variety fraud remained to be seen.

"What about the other household staff?" I asked.

"Clean as a whistle, all of them. Helen Foster has worked for legitimate families for twenty years, never had so much as a traffic ticket. James Morrison, the groundskeeper, is a Vietnam vet with a clean record and steady employment history. Ruth Webb is a single mother working three jobs to support her kids. None of them have financial problems that would make them desperate enough to commit murder."

The contrast between the household staff's clean records and Maya's suspicious background was striking. Walter had surrounded himself with loyal, trustworthy employees for decades, making Maya's rapid rise to a position of such influence even more suspicious.

The office door opened, and Heather walked in carrying a cup of coffee and looking like she'd had a long day. "Sorry I'm late. Traffic was a nightmare coming back from downtown."

"How'd it go with the Brennan siblings?" I asked.

Heather settled into the remaining chair and pulled out her notebook. "Enlightening. Lisa Brennan is genuinely terrified for her father, but she's also desperate enough to do something stupid if she gets cornered."

"What do you mean?"

"She's been calling her father every day, sometimes multiple times, trying to check on him. Maya Santos has been screening the calls, telling Lisa that her father is sleeping or having a bad day. When Lisa does get through, the conversations are brief and Walter seems confused about when they last talked."

"Isolation tactics," I said. "It's a classic pattern in elder abuse cases."

"Lisa admitted she's been considering hiring a lawyer to contest her father's competency," she continued. "She's convinced Maya is drugging him to keep him compliant."

"Based on what evidence?" I asked.

"Mostly instinct and desperation," Heather replied. "But she did mention something interesting. About three weeks ago, she drove out to the house unannounced and found her father in the garden, apparently talking to himself. When she got closer, she realized he was practicing a conversation. He was rehearsing what to say to his lawyer about changing his will."

That was significant. "Rehearsing?" I asked, frowning.

"Like someone had coached him on what to say. Lisa said it didn't sound like her father's words, more like he was reciting a script. But when she asked him about it, he got agitated and claimed he didn't know what she was talking about."

"Did she confront Maya about it?" I said.

"She tried, but Maya had a reasonable explanation. She said Walter had been anxious about the will change and was just working through his feelings about it. She claimed it was actually healthy for him to process his emotions verbally."

The incident suggested that Maya might have been coaching Walter on what to say to justify his will change, preparing him to deflect questions from family members or legal professionals who might question his mental competency.

I made a note. "What about the brother?"

Heather's expression darkened. "Mark Brennan is a desperate man trying very hard to pretend everything is fine. He insisted the family drama was just Lisa being paranoid, that Maya was probably a saint for putting up with their father's difficult personality."

"But?" I said.

"But he's scared. Really scared. He tried to hide it, but I could see the fear in his eyes when he talked about his financial situation. He admitted the restaurant failure hit him hard, but claimed he was 'working with his creditors' to resolve his debts."

"Did he mention Tommy Torrino?" I asked.

"Not by name, but he got very nervous when I asked about his creditors. He started sweating, changing the subject, classic signs of someone who's in over their head."

The fear was understandable, given Tommy Torrino's reputation for his violent collection methods. Mark was living under the constant threat of serious physical harm, which could drive someone to desperate measures.

"Did he seem like he knew about his father's will change?" I asked.

"He knew, all right," heather replied. "And he's furious about it, though he tried to hide that too. Kept saying he didn't care about the money, that he just wanted his father to be happy. But I could tell he was calculating how much his inheritance would have been worth."

"Enough to pay off Tommy Torrino?"

"With plenty left over. But here's the interesting part: when I asked him about Maya Santos, he got defensive. Not angry defensive, more like protective defensive."

I looked up from my notes. "Protective how?"

"Like he was attracted to her. He kept talking about how professional she was, how devoted to their father, how unfair it was for Lisa to be suspicious of her. I got the impression he might have a thing for Maya."

That opened up some interesting possibilities. If

Mark Brennan was attracted to Maya Santos, she might be playing him against his sister, using his feelings to isolate Walter further from his family. Or he might be working with her for a bigger share of the inheritance.

"Did you ask him directly about his relationship with Maya?" I asked.

"I tried to be subtle about it, but yeah. He claimed they barely knew each other, just exchanged pleasantries when he visited his father. But he blushed when he said it, and his body language suggested otherwise."

"D'you think he's sleeping with her?"

"It's possible. Or maybe he's just wishing he is. Either way, it gives Maya another tool to manipulate the family dynamics."

The romantic angle added another layer of complexity to an already complicated situation. Maya Santos was proving to be far more sophisticated in her manipulation techniques than a simple opportunistic caregiver.

The pieces were starting to come together, and none of them painted a pretty picture. Maya Santos was a woman with a history of befriending elderly clients who died and left her money. She was living beyond her apparent means and making mysterious cash payments to someone. She'd isolated Walter Brennan from his family, convinced him to change his will, and now she was potentially using his son's attraction to her to further divide the family.

"There's something else," Heather said. "Mark mentioned that his father has been having 'episodes' lately. Times when he seems confused, disoriented, sometimes doesn't recognize people he's known for years."

"Episodes that conveniently happen when family members are around?"

"That's what Lisa thinks," Heather replied. "She said Maya always has an explanation: he's tired, stressed, having a reaction to his medications. But the episodes seem to coincide with visits from his children."

"What about when Maya's not around?" I asked.

"That's just it; Maya's always around now. She moved into the house about two months ago. She claims Walter needs round-the-clock care. But according to Mark, his father was living independently just fine before Maya came along."

I thought about our visit to the Brennan estate, Walter's moment of clarity when he talked about his business success, the way he'd seemed to gain strength when discussing his concerns about being poisoned. Either he was having good days and bad days, or someone was controlling when he appeared lucid.

"Did either of them mention Dr. Walker?" I asked.

"Lisa did. She's frustrated because Dr. Walker keeps dismissing her father's concerns as paranoid delusions. Says the doctor won't order comprehensive testing and seems more interested in prescribing sedatives than finding out what's wrong."

"And Mark?" I asked.

"He thinks Dr. Walker is great. He said she's been very patient with their father's 'difficult behavior' and has been working closely with Maya to manage his care."

More red flags. If Dr. Walker was legitimate, she should be taking Walter's concerns seriously, especially given his detailed documentation of symptoms. That she was refusing to order toxicology tests suggested either incompetence or complicity.

"All right," I said, "here's what we're going to do. Jacque, I want you to dig deeper into Maya Santos's background. Find out who she really is, where she really went to school, and to who she's been paying five thousand a month. Also, see what you can find about her previous clients: newspaper obituaries, family statements, anything that might give us more details about how they died."

Jacque nodded and made notes.

"Heather, I want you to do some surveillance on Maya. Find out where she goes when she's not at the Brennan house, who she talks to, what her daily routine looks like. If she's running a con, she might have partners or other victims we don't know about."

"What about the Brennan siblings?"

"Keep an eye on them too, especially Mark," I said. "If he's as desperate as he seems, he might do something stupid. And if he's involved with Maya romantically, that could complicate everything."

"What's your next move?" Heather asked.

"I'm going to have a chat with Dr. Walker. If she's Walter Brennan's doctor, she should be concerned about his symptoms and willing to order comprehensive testing. If she's not..."

"You think she's part of whatever Maya's planning?"

I shook my head. "Probably not, but I do think she takes more notice of what Maya Santos tells her than she should."

Jacque looked up from her notes. "What about the samples Walter collected? Are you going to have them tested?"

"I've already arranged it. I'm dropping them off at an independent lab tomorrow morning. We should have results within a week."

"And if they come back positive for toxins?" Jacque asked.

"Then we call Kate and turn this into a police matter," replied. "But if they come back negative, we'll need to figure out whether Walter's symptoms are natural or if whoever is poisoning him is using something that won't show up in standard tests."

"There are plenty of plant-based toxins that are hard to detect," Heather said. "Especially if they're given in small doses over time."

"Which is why I want to know more about Maya's background," I said. "If she has medical training, she'd know exactly how to poison someone without leaving obvious traces."

The office fell quiet as we each considered the implications. Elder abuse was always ugly, but this case had the potential to be much worse. If Maya Santos was systematically murdering elderly clients for their money, Walter Brennan might not be her last victim.

"There's one more thing," I said. "I want everyone to be careful. If Maya Santos is willing to kill for money, she won't hesitate to eliminate anyone who threatens her operation. We need to gather evidence, but we also need to stay alive long enough to use it."

Heather nodded grimly. "How much time do you think Walter has?"

"Hard to say," I replied. "If Maya's following her usual pattern, she'll wait until she's sure the will is legally solid and Walter's family is completely isolated from him. But if she feels threatened, if she thinks we're getting too close..."

"She might speed up her timeline," Jacque finished.

"Exactly. Which means we need to move fast. Walter Brennan's life might depend on how quickly we can expose whatever Maya Santos is really up to."

As my team prepared to leave, I thought about the old man sitting in his mansion, surrounded by people he couldn't trust, slowly losing his health and possibly his life to someone who was supposed to be caring for him. It was a betrayal of the most fundamental kind, using someone's vulnerability and need for help as a weapon against them.

If Maya Santos was what I suspected she was, could we figure out her game before Walter Brennan became her latest victim? Given what Jacque had discovered about her previous clients, time was running out faster than any of us wanted to admit.

But then again, that's what made the job interesting. The cases that mattered were never easy, and the people we usually dealt with were usually the ones who'd run out of other options.

Walter Brennan's daughter had hired us to find out

if someone was trying to kill him. By tomorrow, we'd know if he was right to be afraid.

———

THAT EVENING, after Jade had been tucked into bed with her usual requests for "just one more story" and "five more minutes," I found Amanda in our living room, curled up on the couch with a cup of tea and a stack of news scripts she was reviewing for the next day's broadcast. The domestic tranquility was a welcome contrast to the tension I'd been feeling since my meeting with Lisa Brennan earlier that day.

"Rough day?" Amanda asked, setting aside her scripts as I settled beside her. After almost ten years of marriage, she could read the signs.

I filled her in on Lisa's concerns about her father and Maya Santos, the family dynamics, and the nagging feeling I had that something wasn't quite right about the situation, even though I couldn't put my finger on what it was.

Amanda listened thoughtfully, her years of investigative journalism helping her process the human elements of the story. "You know, Harry," she said, her green eyes narrowed, head tilted to one side, "we've done several segments on elder abuse over the years, and what you're describing fits a classic pattern. An isolated elderly person, strained family relationships, and a caregiver who gradually gains more control over their daily life."

"You think his fears might be legitimate, then?"

She shrugged. "I think his isolation is the bigger concern," Amanda replied. "When we researched those stories, we learned that elderly people who are estranged from their families become prime targets for all kinds of exploitation. If this Maya Santos really is manipulating him, his estrangement from his children makes him the perfect victim. No one's paying close enough attention to notice the gradual changes in his condition or behavior."

Her insight resonated with something that had been bothering me about the case. Walter Brennan was worried not only about his caregiver; he was also trapped in a situation where his concerns weren't being taken seriously by anyone who could help him.

4

THE CAREGIVER'S STORY

I CALLED MAYA SANTOS THE NEXT MORNING AND ASKED if she could meet me at my office. I wanted her away from Walter Brennan's house, away from her familiar territory where she felt she was in control. People revealed more about themselves when they were slightly off balance, and I had a feeling Maya Santos had plenty to reveal.

The morning was crisp and clear, with the kind of autumn light that made Chattanooga look particularly beautiful. From my office windows, I could see the Tennessee River winding through the valley, its surface reflecting the changing leaves on the surrounding hills. It was the kind of day that normally lifted my spirits, but the Brennan case had left me feeling uneasy.

She arrived promptly at ten o'clock, dressed in civilian clothes this time—a tasteful navy blue dress that probably cost more than most caregivers made in a month. Her hair was down, falling in soft waves around her shoulders, and she'd taken time with her makeup. She looked more like a successful business-woman than someone who spent her days caring for an elderly invalid.

The transformation from the professional caregiver I'd met at the Brennan estate was remarkable. Gone were the medical scrubs and the pulled-back hair that gave her an air of clinical competence. In their place was an outfit that spoke of prosperity and sophistication, raising questions about how a private caregiver could afford such expensive clothing and accessories.

"Thank you for coming in, Ms. Santos," I said, gesturing to the chair across from my desk. "I know this situation must be difficult for you."

"It is," she replied, settling gracefully into the chair. "I've been caring for Mr. Brennan for six months, and I've grown very fond of him. It's heartbreaking to see his children turn against him when he needs their support most."

It was an interesting opening move. She was positioning herself as Walter's protector and his children as the villains; a classic manipulation tactic—get your audience to see you as the victim before they start asking difficult questions.

Her body language was relaxed and confident, suggesting someone comfortable with being questioned. Either she was genuinely innocent and had nothing to hide, or she was experienced enough at deception to maintain her composure under pressure.

"Tell me about your relationship with Mr. Brennan," I said. "How did you come to work for him?"

"I was contacted by Premier Home Care Services.

They said they'd received a call from someone requesting care for an elderly gentleman who was having difficulty managing his daily activities. When I met Mr. Brennan, I could see he was struggling. His house was getting cluttered, he was forgetting to take his medications, and he seemed very isolated."

"Who called the agency?"

Maya hesitated for just a fraction of a second. "Mr. Brennan did, of course. He realized he needed help but was too proud to ask his children."

But yesterday Walter had seemed confused about making that call, and Lisa had said her father had never mentioned contacting an agency. Either Walter was more confused than he appeared, or Maya was lying about how their relationship started.

The slight hesitation before her answer was telling. In my experience, people who were telling the truth didn't need time to formulate responses to straightforward questions about how professional relationships began.

"What was your impression of his mental state when you first met him?"

"Declining, but not severely. He was forgetful, sometimes confused about dates or recent events, but still capable of making his own decisions. The isolation was the biggest problem—he'd been withdrawing from social contact since his wife died."

"And his physical health?" I asked.

"Poor," she replied. "He wasn't eating regularly, wasn't taking his medications on schedule, and he'd had several minor falls. That's why I gradually increased my hours. He needed more supervision than we initially thought."

Maya leaned forward slightly, her expression earnest. "Mr. Starke, I want you to understand something. I never asked to live in Mr. Brennan's house. It happened gradually, out of necessity. First, I stayed late when he had a bad episode, then overnight when he was too anxious to be alone, then permanently when it became clear he needed round-the-clock care."

Her explanation sounded reasonable, but the gradual expansion of her presence in Walter's life followed a classic pattern in elder abuse cases. What started as professional assistance had evolved into complete control over his environment and daily routine.

"What kind of episodes?" I asked.

"Panic attacks, mostly. He'd become convinced someone was trying to break into the house, or that his food was poisoned, or that his children were plotting against him. Dr. Walker said it was fairly common in elderly patients. Paranoid ideation brought on by isolation and cognitive decline."

She was good. I had to give her that. Every answer was reasonable, every explanation plausible. If I didn't know about her previous clients and their convenient deaths, I might have believed her without further thought.

"Mr. Brennan claims he's been saving samples of food and medication because he believes someone is poisoning him," I said. "What's your take on that?"

Maya sighed, and for the first time she looked

genuinely sad. "It breaks my heart. He's so convinced that someone is trying to hurt him he won't eat properly, won't take his medications consistently. The paranoia is literally making him sick."

"But you've never had his symptoms investigated medically?"

"Of course I have," she replied. "Doctor Walker has run a comprehensive battery of tests: blood work, urinalysis, even imaging studies. Everything comes back to normal for a man his age. The symptoms he describes are consistent with anxiety, poor nutrition, and medication non-compliance."

"What about toxicology screening?" I asked, watching her carefully.

"Doctor Walker didn't feel that was necessary. Mr. Brennan's symptoms don't match any known poisoning syndrome, and there's no evidence that anyone has access to toxins or reason to use them."

I made a note. "Tell me about his relationship with his children."

Maya's expression hardened slightly. "It's complicated," she said. "Lisa and Mark have been estranged from their father for years. They disagree with his business practices, disapprove of his lifestyle, and they've made it clear they're only interested in their inheritance."

"That seems harsh," I said.

"Is it?" She frowned. "When was the last time either of them visited just to spend time with him? When did they last call without asking for money or complaining about something? Mr. Brennan feels abandoned by his own children, and frankly, I don't blame him."

The criticism of Walter's children was pointed and specific, suggesting Maya had given considerable thought to their relationship with their father.

"But they claim you've been limiting their access to him," I said.

"I've been protecting him from unnecessary stress," she replied, a little haughtily, I thought. "Every time Lisa visits, she interrogates him about his health, his finances, his will. Every time Mark calls, it's because he needs money or wants to complain about his business failures. These interactions leave Mr. Brennan agitated and depressed for days."

Maya sat back in her chair, her composure still perfect despite the serious accusations we were discussing. "Mr. Starke, I understand why his children are suspicious of me. I'm young, I'm attractive, and I have influence over their father. But I earned that influence by being there for him when they weren't. I earned his trust by caring about his welfare more than his wealth."

"Speaking of his wealth, let's talk about the change to his will," I continued.

"What about it?"

"At the very least," I said, "it's unusual for someone to leave their entire estate to a caregiver they've known for only six months."

Maya's eyes flashed, but her voice remained calm. "Mr. Brennan made that decision on his own. I never asked for anything, never even hinted that I expected to be included in his will. When he told me what he'd done, I tried to talk him out of it."

"But you didn't refuse the inheritance."

"Would you? An elderly man with no close family relationships wants to leave his money to someone who's cared for him, someone who's been loyal and devoted. Why should I refuse the gift?"

"Because it creates a powerful motive for murder," said, watching her eyes.

The words hung in the air between us, and for the first time, Maya's composure cracked slightly. Her eyes narrowed, and when she spoke, there was an edge to her voice.

"Are you accusing me of something, Mr. Starke?"

"I'm exploring all the possibilities," I replied, easily. Mr. Brennan believes someone is poisoning him. His children are concerned about his mental competency and possible financial exploitation. You're the person with access to his food and medications, and you're the primary beneficiary of his will. It's natural to ask questions."

Maya stood up, her movements sharp with controlled anger. "I've devoted my life to caring for elderly people. I've given up my personal relationships, my social life, my apartment, to provide round-the-clock care for Mr. Brennan. And this is how I'm repaid? With suspicion and accusations?"

"Sit down, Ms. Santos. I'm not accusing you of anything yet. I'm just trying to understand the situation."

She remained standing for a moment, then slowly

resumed her seat. When she spoke again, her voice was steady but cold.

"What exactly do you want to know?"

"Tell me about your previous clients," I said quietly.

"What about them?"

"Four elderly clients in three years, all of whom died while you were caring for them. That's an unusual pattern."

Maya's face went pale, but she recovered quickly. "Elderly people die, Mr. Starke. That's why they need caregivers. I specialize in end-of-life care, in helping people maintain their dignity and comfort during their final months or years. Death is part of the job."

"And they all happened to leave you money," I said.

"Some did. Not all, and not large amounts. It's not uncommon for grateful clients to remember their caregivers in their wills, especially when they don't have close family relationships."

"Fifty thousand from Margaret Willis. Seventy-five thousand from Robert Myers. One hundred thousand from Dorothy Hamilton. Sixty thousand from James Harrison. That's nearly three hundred thousand dollars in three years."

Maya's composure slipped again, and I could see fear behind her eyes. "You've been investigating me."

"It's what I do, Ms. Santos. And what I've found raises some interesting questions. Like why you're living beyond your apparent means, and why you're making large cash payments to someone every month."

"My finances are none of your business," she snapped.

"They are when they suggest a pattern of financial exploitation. They are when an elderly man believes he's being poisoned and you're the primary beneficiary of his eighty-million-dollar estate."

Maya stood up again, this time grabbing her purse. "I don't have to listen to this. I came here in good faith to help you understand Mr. Brennan's situation, and you're treating me like a criminal."

"Where are you going?" I asked.

"Back to work. Mr. Brennan needs me, even if his children and their hired investigators don't appreciate what I do for him."

"Ms. Santos, if you're innocent, cooperation is in your best interest. If you're not…"

She turned back to face me, and for just a moment, I saw something dangerous in her expression. It was gone so quickly I might have imagined it, but it reminded me that cornered animals could be dangerous.

"I'm innocent of any wrongdoing, Mr. Starke. But I'm not naïve enough to think that matters when there's money involved. Mr. Brennan's children want their inheritance, and they'll destroy anyone who stands in their way."

"Including their father?"

"Ask them, why don't you?"

She walked out, leaving me with more questions than answers. Maya Santos was either an innocent caregiver being unfairly persecuted, or she was one of the most dangerous people I'd ever encountered. Her story was plausible, her explanations reasonable, but something about her felt wrong. Maybe it was the way she'd positioned herself as the victim while simultaneously controlling every aspect of Walter Brennan's life. Maybe it was that flash of something predatory I'd seen in her eyes when she felt threatened.

I picked up the phone and called Tim. "I need you to dig deeper into Maya Santos. Financial records, her employment history, anything you can find."

"How deep are we talking?"

"Deep enough to find out who she really is and what she's really up to. And Tim? Be careful. If I'm right about this woman, she's extremely dangerous."

After I hung up, I sat back in my chair and thought about Maya's visit. She'd come across as professional, caring, and slightly wounded by the family's suspicions. But she'd also been evasive about how she'd initially contacted Walter Brennan, defensive about her previous clients' deaths, and obviously uncomfortable when I'd mentioned her financial situation.

Most telling was her reaction to being questioned. Innocent people got angry when falsely accused, but they also tried to clear their names by providing evidence of their innocence. Maya had done neither. She'd positioned herself as a victim and walked away, which suggested she had something to hide.

My phone buzzed with a text from the lab where I'd sent Walter's samples. "Preliminary results will be available tomorrow afternoon. Will call with details."

Tomorrow afternoon might be too late. If Maya Santos felt threatened by our investigation, she might decide to accelerate her timeline. Walter Brennan's paranoid fears about being poisoned might be the only thing keeping him alive. As long as he remained suspicious, he'd be careful about what he ate and drank. But if Maya convinced him his fears were unfounded, if she managed to drug him into compliance...

I picked up the phone again and called Kate.

"Harry! To what do I owe this honor?"

"I need a favor, Kate. Can you run a check on an elderly man? I'm worried he might be in immediate danger."

"What kind of danger?"

"The kind that comes from trusting the wrong person with your life."

As I explained the situation, I hoped we weren't already too late. Maya Santos had been playing this game for years, and she was very good at it. But she'd made a mistake. She'd picked a victim whose daughter was willing to fight for him.

"I'll be right over," Kate replied.

5

PROFESSIONAL OPINIONS

KATE ARRIVED AT MY OFFICE AN HOUR AFTER I CALLED her, looking like she'd rather be anywhere else. She had that slightly harried expression cops get when they're being pulled in multiple directions at once, and, as always, Samson was at her side.

Samson was a rescue dog, sort of. Kate rescued Samson, a 115-pound long-haired German shepherd, from a near death situation. He was found guarding his murdered master and was about to be shot by one of the uniformed officers when Kate stepped in and rescued him. He's six or seven years old and has obviously had police training at some time in the past, though when and where and by whom she's not been able to discover. He's smart. He can read a room and can quickly assess those who might be of questionable character. That day he was wearing his honorary K-9 harness and badge and, on entering the building, he ran from office to office, greeting his friends with a paw or a lick before returning to Kate's side in my office.

The afternoon heat was building outside, creating the kind of oppressive atmosphere that made everyone slightly on edge. Through my office windows, I could see the heat shimmer rising from the asphalt parking lot, distorting the air and making the distant mountains look like they were wavering in a mirage.

"This better be good, Harry," she said as she sat down in front of my desk. "I've got three active cases and a district attorney who thinks detectives should be able to solve murders with telepathy and good intentions."

I've known Captain Kate Gazzara for more than 22 years, since she was a rookie cop. She made detective in 2003 and was assigned to me as my partner. We've been friends ever since... More than friends, actually, until I screwed it up, but that's another story. Kate's a classic beauty. She, five-eleven, has long, dark blonde hair, a high forehead, an oval face with high cheekbones, and hazel eyes. On occasion, she can be the nice girl with the bright smile and easygoing attitude everyone loves, but she's also a cop. A tough, intimidating, no nonsense cop that nobody dares to fool with.

"Oh, it's good," I replied, as I sat down behind my desk. "And it might be about to become really bad if we don't move fast."

Kate settled back into the chair and pulled out her notebook. Despite her complaints, I could see the professional interest in her eyes. She'd been a cop long enough to recognize when someone was genuinely worried about a potential victim.

"Tell me about Walter Brennan," she said.

I walked her through everything we'd learned: the change to his will, Maya Santos's suspicious background, Walter's claims about being poisoned, and our concerns about possible elder abuse. Kate listened without interruption, making notes and occasionally asking for clarification.

Her questions were precise and professional, cutting through the emotional aspects of the case to focus on the legal and investigative elements that would matter in court. It was a reminder that whatever we discovered about Maya Santos and her activities, we'd ultimately need evidence that would satisfy the criminal justice system.

"So what do you need from me?" she asked when I finished.

"Your perspective on this situation. You've dealt with elder abuse cases. Does this fit the pattern?"

Kate leaned back in her chair, obviously considering her answer. "Actually, we've had some contact with the Brennan household already," she said. "Several calls over the past two months."

"What kind of calls?" I asked.

"Two for possible break-ins that turned out to be Walter Brennan seeing shadows and hearing noises. The responding officers found no evidence of forced entry and no signs of a disturbance of any kind. It's classic paranoid behavior from an elderly man living alone with declining mental faculties."

"What about the caregiver?" I asked.

"Maya Santos was present both times, very professional and cooperative. She explained that Mr. Brennan had been having episodes of anxiety and paranoia, especially at night. She said his doctor was aware of the situation and adjusting his medications accordingly."

I made notes as Kate talked. The police contacts painted a picture of Maya as a competent, patient caregiver dealing with a difficult patient, which was exactly how she wanted to appear to outside observers.

"Any other contacts?" I asked.

"One wellness check requested by his daughter about a month ago. Lisa Brennan called and said she was concerned because she hadn't heard from her father in several days, which was unusual."

"What did you find?"

"An elderly man having a good day, frankly," she replied. "The responding officers reported he was alert, properly dressed, and seemed well-cared-for. The house was clean, his medications were organized, and Maya explained that he'd been having some bad days but was doing much better."

"Did he seem afraid of Maya?"

"Not at all. If anything, he seemed dependent on her. Officer Rachel Ward's report indicates he kept looking to Santos for reassurance, asking her to explain things to us. Classic behavior for someone with cognitive decline who's found a trusted caregiver."

Kate closed her notebook and looked at me seriously. "Harry, based on our contacts with that household, Maya Santos appears to be a dedicated caregiver dealing with a difficult patient. Walter Brennan's claims about poisoning seem consistent with paranoid delusions, not actual threats."

"But what if the paranoia is being induced? What if someone is actually drugging him to make him appear mentally unstable?"

"That's a pretty sophisticated conspiracy theory," she replied. "Do you have any evidence to support it?"

I had to admit I didn't, not yet. "Other than the pattern with her previous clients, no."

"Elderly people die, Harry," she said, reach down to ruffle Samson's ears. "Caregivers who specialize in end-of-life care are going to have higher client mortality rates. And grateful clients do sometimes leave money to people who've cared for them."

"Four clients, four deaths, four inheritances?"

"Without knowing the specific circumstances of each death, that's not necessarily suspicious. What does Walter's doctor say about his condition?"

"That's what I want to find out next," I replied. "Doctor Walker has been treating him for several years. If there's a legitimate medical explanation for his symptoms..." I trailed off.

"Then you've got a family dispute over money, not a murder plot." She stared at me for a moment, then stood up and said. "Look, I have to go; things to do, people to see. Stay in touch, Harry. Come on, Sammy."

After Kate left, I called Dr. Walker's office and was able to schedule an appointment for that afternoon.

Her practice was in a medical building on Gunbarrel Road, an exceptionally busy area in east Chattanooga. It was the kind of place that screamed competence and respectability. The waiting room was filled with elderly patients, and the receptionist had the patient demeanor of someone who dealt with worried families on a daily basis.

The medical building was one of those modern structures designed to inspire confidence in patients and their families. Everything was clean, well-lit, and efficiently organized, from the marble floors in the lobby to the tasteful artwork on the walls. It was the kind of environment where people came seeking healing and hope, making the possibility of medical misconduct even more disturbing.

Dr. Patricia Walker was a woman in her early fifties, with graying hair pulled back in a practical bun and the kind of calm, professional manner that probably reassured anxious patients and their families. Her office was lined with medical degrees and certifications, and she had the slightly tired look of someone who'd been dealing with difficult cases all day.

Her diplomas were impressive, representing decades of medical training and professional development. The office was organized with the precision of someone who dealt with life-and-death decisions regularly, every item in its proper place, and every document carefully filed. She was dressed in a white lab coat over an expensive gray skirt cut just above the knee and a white blouse.

"Mister Starke, I understand you're investigating

some concerns about Walter Brennan's care. I have to tell you, I'm limited in what I can discuss because of patient confidentiality."

"I understand. His daughter Lisa hired me because she's worried about his claims that someone is poisoning him."

Dr. Walker sighed and leaned back in her chair. "Walter is a challenging patient. He's experiencing cognitive decline that's unfortunately common in men his age. The paranoia, the suspicion of his caregivers and family members, these are textbook symptoms of dementia with paranoid features."

"But is it possible that his symptoms are being caused by actual poisoning?" I asked.

"Anything is possible," she replied, "but highly unlikely. I've examined Walter thoroughly on multiple occasions. His blood work is normal for a man his age, his vital signs are stable, and his symptoms are consistent with age-related cognitive decline."

"What about the specific complaints he's made? Weakness, dizziness, nausea after eating?"

"Those could be caused by a dozen different things. His medications can cause dizziness and nausea. Poor appetite is common in elderly patients, especially those dealing with depression and anxiety. Weight loss often accompanies cognitive decline."

Dr. Walker pulled out a thick file from her desk. "Walter's medical history shows a pattern of increasing paranoia and confusion over the past year. It started gradually: forgetting appointments, repeating questions, becoming suspicious of repair workers and delivery people. The symptoms have progressed to where he now suspects his caregiver and family members of plotting against him."

"Have you considered ordering toxicology tests to rule out poisoning?"

"I have, actually. But Walter's symptoms don't match any known poisoning syndrome. He's not exhibiting the acute symptoms you'd expect from most toxins, and the chronic symptoms he describes are better explained by his existing medical conditions and medications."

"So you don't think comprehensive toxicology screening is necessary?"

Dr. Walker hesitated. "It's not that I don't think it's necessary, it's that I don't think it would be helpful. Most toxicology screens test for common substances like alcohol, recreational drugs, and obvious poisons. If someone were using an exotic plant toxin or an unusual pharmaceutical, standard screening might not detect it."

"But you could order more specific tests if there were symptoms that suggested particular toxins?"

"Of course. But Walter's symptoms are vague and nonspecific. Without knowing what to test for, we'd be conducting expensive tests that are unlikely to yield useful results."

I thought about Walter's carefully saved samples, his detailed documentation of when he felt sick. "What if a patient brought you samples of food and medication they suspected were contaminated?"

"I'd have them tested if the patient insisted, but I'd

also counsel them about the psychological aspects of their concerns. Sometimes the fear of being poisoned is more harmful than any actual toxin."

The answer was professionally reasonable, but also slightly dismissive of Walter's concerns. A more thorough physician might have taken his systematic documentation more seriously, especially given the specificity of his complaints.

There was little more I could say, so I up and left.

After leaving Dr. Walker's office, I drove back to mine, feeling less certain about Walter Brennan's situation. The doctor's explanations were reasonable, her concerns about his mental state seemed legitimate, and the police contacts with the household supported her assessment.

When I got back to the office, Jacque informed me that Tim was waiting for me. I found him in his cave, as we called his office, looking frustrated and tired.

"How'd it go with Walter's samples?" I asked.

"Not great," he replied, shaking his head. "I had them analyzed by two different labs, and the results were inconclusive."

"What do you mean, inconclusive?" I asked, frowning.

"The samples are too old and too degraded for reliable testing. Food samples that have been sitting in containers for weeks develop bacteria and chemical changes that interfere with toxicology screening. The medication samples are better preserved, but even those show signs of deterioration."

"So we can't prove he was being poisoned?"

"We can't prove he wasn't being poisoned either," Tim said. "The testing is just not reliable enough to draw conclusions."

Tim handed me a folder with the lab reports. "Both labs said the same thing. If you suspect ongoing poisoning, you need fresh samples taken within hours of the suspected exposure. These samples might have contained toxins originally, but too much time has passed to detect them."

"What about the patterns Walter documented? The correlation between eating certain foods and feeling sick?"

"Could be real, could be psychological," Tim replied, characteristically shoving his glasses further up the bridge of his nose. "Without reliable test results, we can't know for sure."

I went to my office and sat down at my desk, feeling like we'd hit a dead end. Every professional opinion we'd gotten suggested that Walter Brennan was an elderly man suffering from normal cognitive decline, being cared for by a dedicated caregiver and treated by a competent physician. His claims about being poisoned seemed to be products of paranoid delusions rather than actual threats.

But something still bothered me about this whole situation. Maya Santos's background was suspicious, even if it didn't prove she was a killer. The pattern of clients who died and left her money was unusual, even if it wasn't necessarily criminal. And Walter's systematic documentation of his symptoms suggested someone who was still thinking clearly, despite his supposed mental decline.

I picked up my desk phone, called Tim and asked him to come to my office. He arrived two minutes later, his open laptop on his arm.

"Sit down, Tim," I said. "I want you to keep digging into Maya's background. Focus on her previous clients —how they died, what their families thought about it, whether there were any suspicions that weren't pursued."

"You still think she's dirty?" he asked as he sat down.

"I think she's hiding something. Whether it's murder or just garden-variety fraud remains to be seen."

"What about Dr. Walker?"

"She seems legitimate, but I want you to check her background, too. How long has she been Walter's doctor? What's her relationship with Maya? Are there any other patients they've shared who died under suspicious circumstances?"

"I'm on it. But Harry, what if we're barking up the wrong tree? What if this really is just a family dispute over money, and Walter Brennan is just a confused old man with a devoted caregiver?"

"Then we'll have done our due diligence and protected an innocent woman from false accusations. But if we're right about Maya Santos, if she is running some kind of con or worse…"

"We'll be the only thing standing between Walter

Brennan and a carefully planned murder," he finished for me.

"Exactly," I said. "And given what we know about her previous clients, we can't afford to be wrong."

Gotcha," he said and rose to his feet.

As Tim left to continue his research, I leaned back in my chair, linked my hands together behind my neck, and swiveled my chair slightly so I could stare out the window, thinking about the competing narratives we'd uncovered. On the one hand, we had professional opinions from law enforcement and medical experts suggesting that Walter Brennan was suffering from age-related paranoia and being well cared for by Maya Santos. On the other hand, we had a pattern of suspicious deaths, financial irregularities, and a client who insisted he was being slowly poisoned. And on the third, my gut was telling me something wasn't right.

The truth was probably somewhere in between all three, but without solid evidence, I was operating on suspicion and circumstantial evidence. What I needed was something concrete, a smoking gun that would prove definitively whether Walter Brennan was in danger or just confused.

Unfortunately, smoking guns are rare in elder abuse cases. Most of the time, you had to piece together a pattern from small clues and inconsistencies, but could we find that pattern before it was too late? Good question. One to which I had no answer.

But the stakes were becoming clearer with each passing hour. If Maya Santos was indeed systematically poisoning Walter Brennan, every day we delayed could bring him closer to death. But if we acted precipitously based on insufficient evidence, we could destroy an innocent woman's career and reputation while leaving Walter vulnerable to whatever was really threatening him.

The pressure of making the right decision weighed heavily on my shoulders as I considered our next moves.

6

THE FIRST DEATH

My phone rang at six AM, dragging me out of a restless sleep. It was Kate, and she sounded grim.

The early morning call sent an immediate jolt of adrenaline through my system. In my line of work, calls at that hour never brought good news. I could hear the tension in Kate's voice even through the distortion of the phone connection, and I knew immediately that something significant had happened in the Brennan case.

"Harry, we've got a problem. Helen Foster is dead."

I sat up in bed, instantly awake. "What happened?"

"An apparent heart attack. She was found dead in her apartment about an hour ago by her landlord. And given your concerns about the Brennan situation, I thought you'd want to know immediately."

The timing was too convenient to be coincidental. Helen Foster had been one of the few people in Walter's household who might have been able to provide independent verification of his claims about being poisoned. Her sudden death eliminated a potential witness and left Walter even more isolated.

"I'll be right there," I said, swinging my legs out of bed.

"What is it, Harry?" Amanda asked, sleepily.

"It's Brennan's cook," I replied as I stood up. "She's dead. I have to go. Go back to sleep. I'll call you later."

I took a quick shower, threw on clothes and drove across town to Pine Street, where Helen Foster had lived in a modest apartment building that housed mostly working-class retirees. Police cars lined the street, and I could see Doc Sheddon's SUV parked near the entrance.

The neighborhood was quiet in the early morning light, with the kind of peaceful atmosphere that made sudden death seem even more jarring. Helen's building was well-maintained but clearly designed for people living on limited incomes, a reminder that loyal service to wealthy families didn't always translate into personal prosperity.

Kate met me at the building entrance, looking like she'd been up all night. "The body's on the third floor. The landlord found her when he was doing his rounds. Apparently, her apartment door was slightly ajar. Her body was on the floor just inside."

"Any signs of foul play?" I asked.

"None obvious," she replied. There's a prescription bottle for heart medication on the kitchen table, and the landlord says she'd been complaining about chest pains recently."

We climbed to the third floor, where Helen's apartment door stood open with a uniformed officer posted outside. The apartment was small but meticulously clean, with the kind of careful organization that suggested someone who lived alone and took pride in their space.

Helen Foster was flat on her face, her head resting on her arms as if she'd simply laid down for a nap. Doc Sheddon was crouched at her side. There was a half-eaten bowl of cereal on the kitchen table, a cup of coffee that had gone cold, and a newspaper folded to the crossword puzzle.

The scene looked completely natural, exactly what you'd expect to find when an elderly person with heart problems succumbed to a cardiac event. But the timing made it impossible to dismiss the possibility that Helen's death was connected to whatever was happening at the Brennan estate.

"Hey, Doc. What's the preliminary assessment?" I asked.

Doc stood up, stared down at the body for a moment, then sighed and said, "Classic presentation of cardiac arrest. She's got a history of heart problems and was on medication for arrhythmia. We'll do a full autopsy, but this looks like a natural death."

I walked around the apartment, looking for anything that might suggest Helen's death was connected to the Brennan situation. In her bedroom, I found a small desk with bills and personal papers neatly organized. Nothing seemed out of place or suspicious.

"Kate, this is too convenient," I said.

"Heart attacks happen, Harry. Especially to over-weight women in their sixties with a history of cardiac problems."

"But the timing..." I began.

"It could be coincidental," Kate said with a shrug. "Stress can trigger cardiac events. Maybe she discovered something. If she did, and if she was worried about it, and if she was planning to do something about it, that kind of anxiety could easily precipitate a heart attack."

Kate's explanation was theoretically sound, but it didn't address the broader pattern we were seeing. I don't believe in coincidences, and my gut was telling me something else.

Doc Sheddon joined us in the kitchen. "Liver temp, lividity and rigor suggest she died approximately seven hours ago, so let's say sometime between midnight and three AM. There are no signs of trauma, no sign of a struggle. Her heart medication bottle is nearly empty, which suggests she was taking it as prescribed."

"Any chance this could be induced somehow?" I asked.

"It's possible, I suppose, but difficult to prove," he replied. "Someone with medical knowledge could potentially trigger a cardiac event in a person with existing heart problems, but it would require specific drugs and timing."

"What kind of drugs?" Kate asked.

"High doses of cardiac medications, certain stimulants, even some common substances if given in large enough quantities. But without obvious evidence of poisoning, and given her medical history, natural causes is the most likely explanation."

Kate and I left the apartment and walked to a quiet corner of the parking lot. "Harry, I know you're suspicious about this whole situation," she said, "but sometimes a heart attack is just a heart attack."

"I know," I replied. "But I want to talk to Walter Brennan. "You want to come?"

"Sure," she replied, not quite rolling her eyes, but I knew her well enough to know what she was thinking. We were wasting precious time.

It was almost eight in the morning when we arrived at the Brennan estate, where Maya Santos answered the door, looking appropriately shocked and saddened by the news of Helen's death.

"Oh my God," she said, pressing a hand to her chest. "Helen was fine yesterday when she left. She seemed a little tired, but she'd been working extra hours to help with Mr. Brennan's care."

"How is Mr. Brennan handling the news?" I asked.

"He's devastated. Helen was like family to him. She'd been with them for fifteen years. He's convinced that something terrible is happening."

Maya led us to the library, where Walter Brennan sat in his usual chair looking older and more fragile than ever. His eyes were red-rimmed, and his hands shook as he looked up at us.

The grief on Walter's face was unmistakable and heartbreaking. Helen's death had clearly hit him hard.

"They killed her," he said without preamble. "They killed Helen because she knew the truth."

"Mr. Brennan," Kate said gently, "Helen died of a heart attack. There's no evidence that anyone hurt her."

"You don't understand," Walter replied, his voice stronger than his appearance suggested. "Helen came to see me yesterday afternoon. She was scared, really scared. She said she'd figured out what was happening to me, and she was going to call Lisa and tell her everything."

"What had she figured out?"

"That Maya has been poisoning me. Helen said she'd been watching, documenting things, and she'd discovered how it was being done."

Maya stepped forward, her expression pained. "Mr. Brennan, we've discussed this. Your paranoia is getting worse, and now it's extending to poor Helen's death. She died of natural causes."

"Natural causes?" Walter's voice rose. "Helen was healthy as a horse. She worked twelve-hour days, never complained about anything. And suddenly she drops dead the night before she was going to expose what you've been doing to me?"

"Mr. Brennan, please try to calm down. This kind of agitation isn't good for your heart."

"My heart is fine," he snapped. "It's everything else you've been doing to me that's the problem."

I studied Walter's face as he spoke. Despite his obvious distress, his thinking seemed clear and his arguments logical. Either he was having a moment of lucidity despite his supposed dementia, or his mental decline had been greatly exaggerated.

"Mr. Brennan, what specifically did Helen tell you she'd discovered?"

"She said she'd been keeping records, like me. Writing down times when I got sick, what I'd eaten, who had access to my food and medications. She said the pattern was clear once you knew what to look for."

"What pattern?" Kate asked, frowning.

"That I only got sick when Maya was the one who prepared or handled my meals. Never when Helen cooked for me, and never when I prepared my own food. Only when Maya was involved."

Maya shook her head sadly. "Mr. Brennan, I'm here every day. Of course you're more likely to feel sick when I'm around... I'm always around. That's not evidence of poisoning, it's just coincidence."

"Helen didn't think it was coincidence. She said she'd figured out how you were doing it, and she was going to prove it."

"Did she tell you how she thought it was being done?" I asked.

"No, she said she needed to gather more evidence first. But she was excited, like she'd solved a puzzle. She said she'd call Lisa this morning and arrange a meeting." Walter's eyes filled with tears. "And now she's dead."

"Mr. Brennan," Kate said, "I understand you're upset about Helen's death. But people die of natural causes all the time. There's no evidence that anyone hurt her."

"There's no evidence because no one's looking for

it," he wailed. "Helen was the only one who believed me, the only one who was trying to help me. And now she's gone."

Maya moved to Walter's side and placed a comforting hand on his shoulder. "Mr. Brennan, I know this is difficult. Helen was a wonderful woman, and we're all going to miss her. But you can't let your grief turn into more paranoid thoughts."

Walter jerked away from her touch. "Don't touch me. Helen figured out what you're doing, and now she's dead. How convenient for you."

"Mr. Brennan, please," she said. "You're making yourself sick with these thoughts."

"I'm already sick," he snapped. "You've been making me sick for months."

The exchange was telling. Walter seemed genuinely convinced that Helen had discovered evidence of his poisoning, while Maya appeared to be trying to manage his emotional state rather than address his specific accusations. Either Walter was suffering from paranoid delusions, or Helen Foster had indeed stumbled onto something that got her killed.

"Maya," I said, "did Helen mention anything to you about concerns regarding Mr. Brennan's care?"

"She expressed some worry about his increasing paranoia," she replied, "but she understood that it was part of his condition. Helen was very loyal to the family, sometimes too loyal. She took Mr. Brennan's accusations too seriously instead of recognizing them as symptoms of his illness."

"Did she ever suggest that his symptoms might have a physical cause?" Kate asked.

"She mentioned it once or twice, but I explained that Dr. Walker had run comprehensive tests and found nothing abnormal. Helen wasn't medically trained and she sometimes misinterpreted normal age-related changes as signs of illness."

After we left the Brennan house, Kate and I sat in my car discussing what we'd learned.

"Walter seems pretty lucid for someone who's supposed to be suffering from dementia," I said.

"Dementia isn't consistent," Kate replied. "People suffering from it can have moments of clarity followed by periods of confusion. And paranoid delusions can be very coherent and even logical."

"But what if he's right?" I asked. "What if Helen discovered something, and her death wasn't natural?"

"Then we'll find evidence of it in the autopsy," she replied. "But Harry, you can't investigate every death that seems conveniently timed. Sometimes coincidences are just that, coincidences."

I shook my head. "You know how I feel about that," I replied. Anyway, I want to dig deeper into Helen's background. If she was conducting her own investigation into Maya Santos, there could be records of what she found."

"What kind of records?" she asked.

"Notes," I replied, "photographs, documentation. Walter said she was keeping records. If she was, we should be able to find them."

Kate was quiet for a moment, then said, "All right.

I'll make sure the apartment is processed thoroughly, and I'll request a comprehensive autopsy and a full tox screen. If there's any evidence that Helen Foster was murdered, we'll find it."

"What about Walter's claims that Helen figured out how Maya was poisoning him?"

"Without Helen to tell us what she discovered, we're just speculating. But if she did find evidence... Well, as you say, it might still be in her apartment or somewhere else where she kept her records."

"I'll talk to Lisa Brennan," I said, "and see if Helen mentioned anything to her about it. And I'll have Tim dig deeper into Helen's background."

As Kate drove away, I couldn't help but think about Helen Foster's death and Walter Brennan's reaction to it. The timing was certainly suspicious, but Kate was right that people died of natural causes all the time, especially older folk. But was Helen's death simply a tragic coincidence, or was it murder?

Either way, Walter Brennan was now more isolated than ever. With his strongest ally dead and his family convinced he was suffering from paranoid delusions, it didn't look good for him. And, if Maya Santos was planning to kill him, it was indeed likely she'd just eliminated the person most likely to expose her plan.

The thought that Helen Foster might have died because she tried to protect Walter Brennan made me more determined than ever to get to the truth. If she'd discovered evidence of Maya's crimes, then her death wouldn't be in vain. But if she'd died of natural causes while trying to save a confused old man from imaginary threats, then we were all wasting time that could be better spent on real crimes and actual victims.

The only way to know for sure was to find out what Helen Foster had discovered, and whether it was worth killing for.

7

HIDDEN HISTORIES

I DIDN'T GET HOME TILL AFTER ELEVEN THAT NIGHT. Amanda was already in bed and asleep, so rather than disturb her, I slept on the couch in the living room. Sleep didn't come easy, though. It never does when I'm dealing with a complex puzzle, and the Brennan case was certainly that. I finally drifted off sometime around one in the morning, only to be awoken when TJ called me at seven-thirty the next morning. He was at the office and he was excited.

"Harry, you need to get down here. I couldn't sleep, so I've been here since five, working on Maya Santos's employment history, and what I found is going to make your hair curl. This case is about to get a lot more complicated."

I sighed, then said, "Give me an hour, TJ." And I hung up.

The early morning light was just beginning to filter through my bedroom windows when I took Amanda a cup of coffee. She was already up and exiting the shower.

"You slept on the couch," she said accusingly. "What was that about?"

"I didn't want to disturb you. I… It's… Look, it's complicated, and I had a lot on my mind. And I just had a call from TJ. I need to go."

"You need to shower first," she replied. "You don't exactly… stink, but you need to freshen up."

She's right, I thought as I reminded myself that I'd gotten precious little sleep worrying about Walter Brennan's safety and Helen Foster's suspicious death. And that TJ's call had only confirmed that my instincts about the case were leading us deeper into dangerous territory. She I took a cold shower, dressed in a clean pair of jeans and a white golf shirt. Then I grabbed a slice of toast and a to-go cup of coffee, kissed my wife and daughter, and hurried out the door.

When I arrived some twenty-five minutes later, Jacque was already there, working at her computer with a stack of legal documents beside her. She looked up as I walked in, her expression troubled, and rose quickly to her feet.

"This is bigger than we thought, Harry," she said without preamble.

"How big?"

"We need to go to TJ's office," she said and walked quickly around me and out into the corridor.

TJ was surrounded by printouts and hit twin computer screens displaying various employment databases and records. He looked like he'd been up all night, which I already knew he hadn't, but his eyes were bright with the satisfaction of a puzzle solver who'd finally found some missing pieces.

"I turned to Jacque and repeated my question, "How big?"

It was TJ who answered. He pulled out a manila folder and opened it on the desk between us. "Maya Santos has worked for at least seven elderly clients over the past four years, not just the handful we initially identified."

"Seven?"

"Seven that I can confirm through employment agencies and placement services. But here's the disturbing part; five of them died while she was providing care."

He handed me a list of names, dates, and locations. "These are the ones that died. Margaret Willis, Atlanta, died 2021. Robert Myers, Birmingham, died 2022. Dorothy Hamilton, Houston, died 2022. James Harrison, Nashville, died 2023. And Patricia Daniels, Memphis, died last year."

"All natural causes?"

"According to the death certificates, yes," Jacque said. "Heart failure, stroke, complications from diabetes, pneumonia, and another heart attack. All believable for elderly people with existing health problems."

I studied the list, noting the geographical spread and timing. The pattern suggested a systematic operation rather than random criminal behavior, with Maya moving from city to city and targeting vulnerable elderly people across the southeastern United States.

"What about the two who didn't die?"

"That's where it gets interesting. Both clients terminated Maya's employment after family members became suspicious of her relationship with their elderly relatives. In both cases, the families complained Maya was isolating their loved ones and asking inappropriate questions about finances."

TJ opened another folder. "I contacted the families of the deceased clients. Three of them were willing to talk to me, and they all had similar concerns."

"Bit early to contact them, wasn't it?" I said. "It's not even nine yet... What kind of concerns?" I asked, staring at him.

He shrugged. "I didn't look at the time. Anyway, it seems Maya gradually isolated the clients from family contact, convinced them their relatives were only interested in money, and encouraged them to make changes to their wills. In each case, the client left substantial sums to Maya; not everything, but significant amounts."

"How much?" I asked.

"We already know about four of them: sixty thousand from James Harrison, fifty thousand from Margaret Willis. Seventy-five thousand from Robert Myers. One hundred thousand from Dorothy Hamilton. Patricia Daniels' family wouldn't discuss financial details, but they confirmed that Patricia had left money to Maya. So five dead; five inheritances"

I leaned back against the wall. My mind was in a

whirl. The pattern was clear. "So Maya Santos has been running the same con for years."

"It looks that way," TJ said. "And Harry, there's something else. In each case where the client died, there were other household employees who had become suspicious of Maya's activities."

"What happened to them?"

"Margaret Willis had a housekeeper who quit suddenly about a month before Margaret died. She moved out of state and refused to talk to me. Robert Myers' groundskeeper died in an accident two weeks after Robert's death. Dorothy Hamilton's cook had a heart attack shortly after Dorothy died."

If Maya Santos was eliminating potential witnesses along with her victims, Helen Foster's death took on a much more sinister significance.

I stared down at TJ. "All of that suggests Maya's been working the con for years," I said. "She finds isolated elderly people, gains their trust, isolates them from their families, and then... what? Kills them?"

"I can't prove that yet. But yes, the pattern is undeniable. Elderly clients die under her care; household staff who might have witnessed suspicious activities either disappear or die of apparent natural causes, and Maya inherits substantial sums of money."

Jacque spoke before I could answer. "Harry. I've been investigating Helen Foster's background, and what I found explains a lot about why she was asking questions about Maya."

"What do you mean? What kind of background?" I asked.

"You're gonna love this: Helen Foster wasn't just a cook. She was a retired private investigator."

I stared at Jacque. "What?"

"She worked for Masterson Investigations in Atlanta for twelve years before moving to Chattanooga five years ago. She specialized in insurance fraud, background checks, and domestic investigations."

Jacque handed me a folder containing Helen's professional history. "She was good at her job, too," she continued. "She was awarded commendations from several insurance companies, and testimonials from attorneys. And she had a clean record with the state licensing board."

"Why did she retire?" I asked.

"Health problems," Jacque replied. "According to her former employer, she had a minor heart attack about six years ago and decided to scale back to less stressful work. That's when she moved to Chattanooga and took the job with the Brennan family."

The pieces were falling into place. Helen Foster had gotten herself a stress-free job and in doing so had stumbled onto a criminal enterprise and, being the trained investigator she was... Well, you get the idea.

"So when Helen became suspicious of Maya—"

"She did what she'd been trained to do," Jacque finished for me. "She started investigating. Quietly, professionally, documenting everything she observed."

"And that means she must have kept records," I said. "Have you found anything?"

"Not directly," Jacque replied. "But I did find some interesting financial transactions. Three months ago,

Helen opened a safe deposit box at First Horizon Bank. She also increased her life insurance policy and named her sister as the beneficiary."

"Sounds like she was preparing for something untoward," I said, thoughtfully."

"That's what it looks like," Jacque said. "And Harry, there's something else. Helen made several phone calls to her former colleagues in Atlanta over the past month. I contacted Masterson Investigations, and they confirmed she'd been asking about resources for investigating caregiver fraud and elder abuse."

TJ leaned back in his chair. "So we've got a retired private investigator who recognized suspicious patterns in Maya Santos's behavior and started conducting a professional investigation. And now she's dead of an apparent heart attack."

"The timing is more than convenient," I said. "Helen dies just as she's building a case against Maya, and Walter loses his only ally who might have been able to expose whatever it was Maya was doing to him."

"But we still don't have proof that Maya killed anyone," Jacque pointed out.

"True," I said. But the pattern you guys have found suggests this isn't random good fortune. Maya Santos has been systematically targeting vulnerable elderly people, and people who might expose her activities have a tendency to die or disappear."

I thought about Walter Brennan, sitting in his mansion with Maya Santos, believing he was being slowly poisoned but unable to prove it. If we were right about Maya's history, he was living with someone who was readying herself to kill him. No wonder he was frickin' paranoid.

"So, what's our next move?" TJ asked.

"We need to find out what Helen discovered during her investigation," I said. "If she was the professional her background suggests, she would have documented everything."

"Where would she keep those records?" Jacque asked.

"Somewhere safe, you can bet..." I trailed off, then said, "Jacque, that safe deposit box Helen opened; we need to find out what's in it."

"That'll require a court order. Helen's dead, so we'd need to go through her estate."

"Who's her next of kin?"

"Her sister, Sarah Foster. She lives in Atlanta. I've already contacted her about Helen's death, and she's coming up this weekend to handle the arrangements."

I nodded. "Good! Set up a meeting with Sarah Foster. If Helen was investigating Maya Santos, her sister might know something about it. And if Helen left evidence in that safe deposit box, we need to get access to it legally. She should be able to do that."

"What about Maya?" TJ asked. "Do we confront her with what we've found?"

"Not yet," I replied. "If she really has killed five people and eliminated witnesses, she won't hesitate to kill Walter and disappear if she feels threatened. We need more evidence before we make any moves."

"And Walter?" Jacque asked.

"We keep monitoring his situation," I said. "That's

about the best we can do. If Maya follows her usual pattern, she'll wait until she's sure the will is legally solid, and Walter's family is completely isolated from him. But if she suspects we're closing in..."

"She might speed up her timeline," Jacque finished for me.

"Exactly." I said. "Which means we need to move fast, but carefully. Walter Brennan's life might depend on how quickly we can prove Maya Santos is a serial killer without alerting her to our investigation."

My phone rang, interrupting our planning session. It was Kate, and her voice was grim.

"Harry, we need to talk. There's been a development in the Helen Foster case and you're not going to like it."

"What kind of development?" I asked.

"The kind that suggests Helen Foster's death might not have been as natural as we initially thought. Can you meet me at Doc's?"

"Sure. I'll be there in," I looked at my watch. "Let's say thirty minutes." I hung up and turned to Jacque.

"I need coffee to go. D'you mind?" I asked. "I need a quick word with Tim."

Tim's fingers were flying across his keyboard as multiple screens displayed financial records, bank statements, and credit reports. As always, he'd been working since before dawn, diving deep into the financial backgrounds of everyone connected to the Brennan case, and what he'd found painted a picture of desperation that extended far beyond the family members.

"Harry, you need to see this," he said without

looking up from his monitors as I walked through the door. "Everyone in this case is drowning in debt."

I settled into the chair beside his desk, noting the empty coffee cups and energy drink cans that suggested he'd been pulling an all-nighter. "Start with the Brennan siblings."

"Lisa first," Tim said, pulling up a comprehensive financial profile. "Her art gallery, Brennan Fine Arts, is hemorrhaging money faster than I initially calculated. She's not just three months behind on rent, she owes eight months' totaling forty-two thousand dollars. Her landlord has already filed eviction proceedings."

"Wow," I muttered. "That's worse than we thought."

"Much worse. And the IRS has placed liens on both her business and personal assets for unpaid taxes going back three years. Total owed: seventy-eight thousand in back taxes, plus penalties and interest that push it over ninety thousand."

Tim scrolled through more documents. "Her business loan is in default, credit cards are maxed out at sixty-seven thousand combined, and she's borrowed against her life insurance, her car, and her house. Conservative estimate of her total debt: two hundred and thirty thousand dollars."

"What about income?" I asked.

"The gallery sold exactly three pieces last month for a total of twelve hundred dollars. Her overhead is eight thousand a month. She's got maybe six weeks before complete financial collapse."

"And Mark?" I asked.

Tim's expression darkened as he pulled up another

set of records. "Mark Brennan is in even deeper trouble. The restaurant closure was just the beginning. Total business debts from Morrison's Bistro: three hundred and seventy thousand dollars. But that's not the scary part."

"Tommy Torrino?" I said.

Tim nodded, did his thing with his glasses, then said, "One hundred and fifty thousand to Torrino's organization, plus compound interest that's been running for six months. At their rates, he probably owes close to two hundred thousand by now."

Tim showed me surveillance photos from his database searches. "Torrino's people have been making regular visits to Mark's apartment. Last week, they hospitalized a guy who owed them eighty thousand. Mark owes more than twice that."

"How long d'you think he has before they decide to make an example of him?" I asked.

"Based on Torrino's usual pattern? Maybe two weeks before they make an example of him. Mark Brennan is a dead man walking unless he gets a large sum of money quickly."

I studied the financial records, thinking about the desperation both siblings must be feeling. Lisa facing complete financial ruin and potential jail time for tax evasion, Mark facing probable death at the hands of loan sharks, and both of them with an eighty-million-dollar inheritance just out of reach.

"What about Maya Santos?" I asked.

"That's where it gets really interesting," Tim said, pulling up Maya's financial profile. "On the surface,

Maya should be financially comfortable. Her credit report shows she's received substantial inheritances from previous clients over the past few years. We already knew that. Nearly three-hundred-thousand. But here's what's strange: despite receiving all this money, Maya's current financial situation doesn't reflect it. She's still carrying sixty-eight thousand in student loan debt, and her spending patterns suggest she's living paycheck to paycheck."

"So where did the money go?"

Tim showed me bank records and financial transfers. "That's what I've been trying to figure out. Maya received these large sums, but then she made substantial cash transfers and purchases that are difficult to track."

"What kind of transfers?" I asked, frowning.

"Large cash withdrawals, wire transfers to accounts I can't identify, and purchases of cashier's checks made out to 'cash.' It's like she was systematically moving the money somewhere else."

"Money laundering?" I said.

"That's possible. Or she was being forced to transfer the money to someone else. Look at this pattern; every time Maya received an inheritance, within weeks she'd made transfers that eliminated most of the windfall."

Tim pulled up another screen. "And here's what's really suspicious. About six months ago, right around the time she started working for Walter Brennan, Maya began receiving regular cash deposits of thousand dollars per month."

"Someone's paying her?" I asked.

"The timing suggests she's being paid for her work with Walter, but not by the Brennan family. These payments are coming from an unknown source, always cash, always deposited at the same branch."

"So Maya has a history of inheriting money from elderly clients," I said, "but she's not keeping it. Or... she hiding it. And now someone is paying her cash to work with Walter Brennan."

"That's what the financial records suggest. Either Maya is part of a larger operation that takes most of her inheritance money, or she's transferring the funds offshore, hiding the money."

"Tim, this makes Maya look even more suspicious. She has to be hiding it. Nothing else makes any sense, unless—"

"She's not working alone. The financial transfers and regular payments indicate someone else is involved in whatever scheme she's running."

"What about the household staff?"

"Helen Foster was clean financially," Tim replied. "Modest savings, no debt except a small car loan. And... Oh wait. I almost forgot. She has a storage unit on East Brainerd. You might want to take a look." He handed me a sticky note with the address.

"What about the others?" I asked.

"Jim Morrison, the groundskeeper, has been working for the Brennan family for twenty years. Steady income, modest lifestyle, no debt problems. He lives in the apartment above the garage, so his expenses are minimal."

"And Ruth Webb?"

"Single mother, works two jobs, barely making ends meet. She owes about fifteen thousand in medical bills from when her daughter broke her leg last year. Not desperate money problems, but she's definitely not flush."

I sucked my bottom lip as I processed the financial information Tim had compiled. Everyone connected to the Brennan household was under some sort of financial pressure. Maya Santos's mysterious additional income was puzzling, but it didn't necessarily point to murder.

What was clear was that Walter Brennan's eighty-million-dollar estate represented salvation for two desperate people and riches for a third. His daughter was facing complete financial ruin, his son probable death from loan sharks, and his caregiver standing to inherit the lot.

"Tim, keep digging into Maya. We need to know the who, what and why of those cash deposits she's been making. "

"I'll keep working on it. But Harry, it has to be one of the three. The financial pressure on the children is incredible, and Santos... well, eighty million bucks would be motive enough for one of them to want Walter Brennan dead."

"That's what worries me," I said. "With this much money at stake and these three desperate people involved, someone might be willing to take desperate action."

As I prepared to leave, I thought about the pattern TJ and Jacque had uncovered. It was a stunner. I mean, think about it: Maya Santos had perhaps been killing elderly clients for years, and eliminating witnesses who might expose her activities, and now she was positioning herself to pick up Walter Brennan's eighty-million-dollar empire. You'd have to give her credit for thinking big, if nothing else.

Then, if you want to talk about coincidence, how about Helen Foster PI being the one person in Walter's household with the training and experience to recognize what Maya was doing? The sad thing about it was, her impromptu investigation had probably cost her her life.

So, Maya was out prime suspect. So all we had to do was prove it before she claimed Walter as her next victim, and Helen Foster's death became just another in a series of convenient accidents and natural deaths that had allowed a serial killer to operate with impunity for years. Easy, right? Not hardly.

We were running out of time. Something had to break, and soon.

8

FINANCIAL PRESSURES

I MET KATE AT THE MORGUE IN DOC'S OFFICE, WHERE she was reviewing Helen Foster's autopsy results with him. Samson sat quietly beside her chair, his ears pricked. His mouth opened and his tongue lolled out when he saw me enter the room.

Kate looked up at me, her expression grim.

"What's up?" I asked.

"The autopsy results," she replied. Doc found something. Helen Foster was murdered."

Doc gestured to the report in front of him and nodded. "Herry, my friend. What Kate said is true. Helen Foster didn't die of a simple heart attack as we initially thought. The cardiac arrest was caused by digitalis toxicity. She was given a massive dose that would have been fatal within minutes."

"Digitalis? The same substance we suspected Walter is being poisoned with?"

"Exactly," he replied. Someone injected Helen with a concentrated digitalis solution. The injection site in her neck is so small it was missed during the initial examination."

Kate leaned forward. "Harry, Helen Foster was murdered."

"Yeah, I got that," I replied. "I guess she was getting too close to the truth about Maya's activities."

"Or she discovered something that threatened the entire operation," Kate replied. Either way, this changes things. I called the chief, and it's now officially my case."

"That figures," I said with a grin. Then I looked at Doc and said, "How long would Helen have survived after the injection?"

"Minutes at most," he replied. "Digitalis in that concentration causes almost immediate cardiac arrest. She probably didn't even realize what was happening."

Kate stood up. Samson rose too. "I need to get back to the office," she said. "I'll talk to—"

"Wait," I said. "There's something else. Helen had a storage unit on East Brainerd. I think we should take a look. She might have kept her evidence there. You want to go take a look? If Helen documented Maya's activities or discovered proof of systematic poisoning, we need to find it before someone else does. I think Helen was murdered to silence her. I also think if Maya knew about the unit she'll want to go after it. We need to get to it before she does."

She nodded, then said, "She also had a safe deposit box at First Horizon. We should take a look at that, too. But, Harry, we don't know for sure that it's Maya, Harry. It could be one of the kids."

"All the more reason we get to it before they do," I said.

Kate nodded. I handed her the sticky note with the address. She took out her phone and called Corbin Russell, her partner, and told him to go straight to Judge Strange and get a warrant for the storage unit and the safe deposit box and then meet us at the unit.

"I should have the paperwork within an hour. I need to go back to my office. Do you want to meet me at the unit?"

"Absolutely. I need to get something to eat. I'll meet you there in an hour."

Kate's office was three blocks from Doc's little house of horrors—the Hamilton County Forensics Department—so she didn't have far to go. Me? I made a beeline for the nearest Hardees, where I ordered two sausage and egg biscuits and a large coffee to go. Then I called TJ and asked him to meet me at the facility.

THE STORAGE FACILITY was one of those sprawling complexes on the edge of town where people kept the things they couldn't bear to throw away but didn't want cluttering up their homes. Rows of identical metal buildings stretched across several acres, separated by narrow access roads and monitored by security cameras that probably worked about half the time. The place had the desolate feel of a graveyard for discarded dreams and forgotten possessions.

Helen Foster's unit was in building C, number 247.

Kate had obtained a search warrant based on the suspicious circumstances of Helen's death and her potential connection to our investigation. The paperwork had taken most of the morning, but Judge Strange, a personal friend of my family, had agreed that Helen's background as a private investigator warranted a thorough examination of her stored belongings. Samson sat patiently beside Kate's car while we waited for the facility manager to arrive with the key. He would be the first to enter. If there was anything dangerous inside, he would find it..

"The unit's been paid up through the end of the year," the manager said as he unlocked the roll-up door. He was a thin man in his fifties who looked like he'd spent too many years dealing with other people's unwanted possessions. "Miss Foster was real particular about that. Paid six months in advance, said she didn't want to worry about late fees. Most folks around here pay month to month, but she insisted on the long-term deal."

The door rolled up with a metallic screech to reveal a disappointingly ordinary storage space. A few boxes of what looked like personal belongings, some old furniture covered with dusty sheets, and a small filing cabinet pushed against the back wall. Whatever I'd been hoping to find—surveillance equipment, investigation files, evidence of Helen's professional activities —this wasn't it. The space felt more like a shrine to a previous life than an active investigation headquarters. Nevertheless, Kate sent Samson in to do his thing.

The big German Shepherd moved methodically

through the unit, his nose working to detect anything unusual, but his body language remained relaxed rather throughout. His training, so we thought, had probably covered drugs, explosives, and large quantities of cash, because, in the past, he'd managed to sniff out all three, but nothing here triggered his specialized responses. He found nothing and came out with his tail between his legs, obviously disappointed.

"Not exactly the secret command center I was expecting," TJ said, stepping into the unit and surveying the modest collection of stored items.

"Mostly personal papers and old tax returns," I said, going through the filing cabinet drawer by drawer. The documents were neatly organized but mundane—utility bills from her Atlanta apartment, medical records, insurance policies. "Nothing that looks like an investigation into Maya Santos or anything related to the Brennan family."

TJ opened one of the boxes and found some photo albums, old letters, and memorabilia from Helen's previous life in Atlanta. Wedding photos showed a younger Helen with a man who must have been her late husband. Family gatherings, vacation snapshots, the accumulated visual history of a life that had been interrupted by tragedy and relocated to Chattanooga. "Looks like she used this place to store memories, not evidence."

Kate was examining an old desk that had been Helen's only furniture in the unit, methodically pulling out drawers and checking for hidden compartments or false bottoms. "There might be something here," she said, running her hands along the interior surfaces. "But it's not obvious. If Helen was hiding professional materials, she was better at it than most people."

"Maybe we were wrong about Helen conducting a professional investigation," I said, disappointed that a promising lead had failed to deliver. "Maybe she was just a concerned employee who got suspicious about Maya's behavior and started paying closer attention."

"Or maybe she was smarter than we gave her credit for," Kate replied, continuing her examination of the desk's construction. "If she was investigating something dangerous, she wouldn't keep the evidence in a storage unit that could be traced back to, not if she was a professional, which she obviously was ."

We spent another hour going through everything in the unit, examining each box thoroughly and checking every piece of furniture for hidden compartments or concealed documents. But we found nothing that suggested Helen Foster had been conducting a systematic investigation into Maya Santos or anyone else connected to the Brennan household. If she had discovered something that got her killed, she'd hidden it somewhere else entirely, perhaps in a location that couldn't be connected to her identity.

As we prepared to leave, TJ made one final discovery in a box of Helen's personal papers that we'd initially dismissed as unimportant. "This might be something," he said, holding up a small address book with a worn leather cover. "Helen kept detailed records of addresses and phone numbers, including several people in other cities. Some of these entries have recent dates."

I examined the address book and found entries for people in Atlanta, Houston, and Birmingham—cities where Maya Santos had previously worked according to her employment history. Next to each name, Helen had made small notations in her cramped handwriting: "MS client 2019," "died 2020," "family suspicious." The entries were cryptic but suggestive of someone tracking patterns across multiple locations and time periods.

"She was tracking Maya's previous employment," I said, studying the notations, trying to decipher their meaning. "But this isn't evidence of murder. It's just a record of where Maya had worked and possibly what had happened to her previous clients."

"Still, it shows Helen was paying attention to the patterns," Kate said, reading over my shoulder. "She might have been building a case based on circumstantial evidence, just not keeping her active investigation files here where they could be easily discovered."

We left the storage facility with more questions than answers, but we still had the safe deposit box. Maybe that would provide the answers we were looking for.

THE FIRST HORIZON'S BANK'S vault felt appropriately somber as Kate and I followed the bank manager, Mrs. Patterson, into the room lined with safe deposit boxes, and I was hoping the delay while we searched the storage unit hadn't given someone else time to somehow access Helen's evidence before us.

"Box 223," Mrs. Patterson said, stopping at a medium-sized compartment near the end of the row. "Ms. Foster opened this account exactly three months ago. She was very specific about the security protocols and paid for two years in advance."

Kate showed her badge and the warrant. "We'll need privacy to examine the contents."

"Of course. I'll be in the lobby if you need anything."

The safe deposit box was significantly larger than I'd expected, and when we lifted the lid, it was clear that Helen had been conducting a far more comprehensive investigation than we'd realized. Unlike the storage unit with its single notebook, the safe deposit box was packed with meticulously organized evidence.

"Geez," Kate said, looking at the contents.

The box contained multiple file folders, each labeled with a different name and date. Margaret Willis, Robert Myers, Dorothy Hamilton, James Harrison, Patricia Daniels—all the names we'd heard associated with Maya's previous clients, plus several others I didn't recognize.

I opened the Margaret Willis file and found medical records, death certificates, copies of will changes, and detailed notes in Helen's careful handwriting documenting the timeline of Maya's employment and the client's declining health.

"Kate, the pattern is the same for every client. Maya gets hired, the client's health mysteriously declines, the will gets changed, the client dies, and Maya inherits a substantial sum."

"And look at this," Kate said, showing me another folder. "Helen also investigated Maya's financial activity after each inheritance."

The financial records showed the same pattern Tim had discovered: Maya would receive substantial inheritances, then quickly transfer most of the money through untraceable transactions. But Helen had gone further, attempting to track where the money was actually going.

"Hmm, it looks like someone was taking Maya's inheritance money," I said, studying Helen's analysis. "Either that or she was laundering the money, but why would she? The inheritances were legal income."

"I think she was being forced to turn them over to someone else," Kate said. "Look at this note Helen wrote."

She handed me a handwritten analysis dated just two weeks before Helen's death. It read, "Maya appears to be working with or for someone else. The inheritances are being funneled to unknown parties through a sophisticated series of financial transfers. Maya may be a front person for a larger operation."

At the bottom of the safe deposit box, we found Helen's most disturbing discovery: a manila envelope marked "Evidence - Poisoning Analysis."

"Hah!" Kate said, opening the envelope to reveal laboratory reports from a private testing facility. "She somehow obtained samples from Maya's previous clients, and she had them independently tested."

The lab results showed traces of an assortment of poisons in hair samples, food residue, and personal items from several of Maya's clients. I shook my head. It didn't look good for Maya.

"It looks like Helen proved that Maya was systematically poisoning her clients," I said, reading through the detailed analysis. "But, Kate, it's all circumstantial. This could be evidence of serial murder, but think about it; anyone could have administered these poisons."

Kate and I looked at each other, and I could tell what she was thinking. Was Maya Santos involved in systematic murder? It certainly looked like it, but something I couldn't quite put my finger on was bugging me. To me, the contents of the box raised more questions than answers.

"Harry," Kate said, finally. "This can't be a coincidence. The contents of this box prove that Maya is a serial killer…" Kate trailed off when she saw the look on my face. Then she frowned and said, "What?"

"I don't know," I replied. "There's something weird going on and I don't know what it is. Maya's smart. There's no doubt about that, but… I dunno. It's all a little in your face, don't you think?"

Kate gave me 'the look,' then said, "And you think what?"

"Yeah, I think Maya might be the one administering the poison, but what if she's not? What then?" I heaved a sigh, shook my head, then said, "You're right. This evidence, circumstantial as it is, cannot be overlooked. But it's not enough to make an arrest. A good defense attorney would get it thrown out during the prelims.

We need to catch her red-handed. Look, I need to… I need to see someone. I'll talk to you later." And with that, I turned and walked out of the room leaving Kate staring after me.

Me? I figured I needed more information and where better to start than with the groundskeeper, James Morrison.

9

THE GROUNDSKEEPER'S SECRETS

I DECIDED TO APPROACH JAMES MORRISON BY MYSELF and directly, rather than going through Maya Santos or any other intermediary. The more I thought about it, the more I realized that if the groundskeeper had been working for the Brennan family for twenty years, he might have observed things that others had missed, and he was probably the only household employee who wasn't under Maya's direct influence or supervision or, more importantly, financial pressure. His long tenure with the family would give him a historical perspective that newer employees lacked.

The Brennan estate grounds were immaculate, a testament to Morrison's skill and dedication. Perfectly manicured lawns were bounded by carefully maintained flower beds, and mature trees provided strategic shade while framing views of the main house.

I found him in the greenhouse behind the main house, tending to what looked like an impressive collection of exotic plants that must have cost thousands of dollars to acquire and maintain. He was a man in his early sixties, weathered from decades of outdoor work but moving with the steady competence of someone who knew his trade intimately.

"Mister Morrison? I'm Harry Starke. I'm investigating some concerns about Mr. Brennan's welfare on behalf of his daughter."

Morrison looked up from the orchid he'd been examining, his expression cautious but not unfriendly. Years of working for wealthy families had probably taught him to be careful about what he said to strangers, but his weathered face suggested someone who was fundamentally honest. "I figured someone would show up eventually," he muttered, as if to himself. "Lisa's been worried sick about her father calling here, asking questions."

"What's your take on the situation?" I asked.

Morrison set down his watering can and wiped his hands on a towel, taking his time before responding. "Mister Brennan's not the same man he was a year ago. He's aged ten years in the past six months, and it's not just his body that's failing. His mind's not as sharp as it used to be."

"How do you mean?"

"His mind comes and goes more than it should for someone his age. Some days he's sharp as ever, remembers things from twenty years ago better than I do, knows every plant in this greenhouse, remembers conversations we had years ago. Other days he doesn't even recognize me, gets confused about where he is, sometimes doesn't even remember his wife is dead."

Morrison gestured toward the main house. His expression seemed troubled. "But the strange thing is, the bad days seem to happen more often when certain people are around. It's not random like you'd expect with normal age-related decline."

"Such as?"

"Well, Maya, mostly. When she first started working here, Mr. Brennan seemed to perk up. He had more energy, was more like his old self. She seemed to be good for him, got him interested in things again. But gradually, that changed. Now when she's hovering around him, he gets confused and agitated."

"Have you mentioned this to anyone?" I asked.

Morrison's expression darkened, and he glanced around as if making sure we weren't being overheard. "I tried talking to Maya about it, suggested maybe Mr. Brennan needed a different approach or maybe some time away from constant supervision. She got defensive, said I didn't understand his medical condition and that I should stick to gardening."

"What about his children?" I said.

"I've known Lisa and Mark since they were kids, watched them grow up on these grounds. They're not perfect, God knows, but they love their father. This idea that they're only interested in his money..." Morrison shook his head with conviction. "That's not the family I've worked for all these years. They have their problems, but they're not heartless."

I studied Morrison's face, looking for signs of deception or hidden motives. His long relationship with the family could make him biased in their favor, but his genuine concern about Walter Brennan's welfare seemed authentic. He seemed genuinely concerned about Walter Brennan's welfare, and his long history with the family gave his observations more weight than those of the newer employees.

"Mister Morrison, have you noticed anything specific about Maya's behavior that concerns you?" I asked.

Morrison was quiet for a moment, clearly considering how much to tell me. He picked up a small pruning tool and absently cleaned it while he thought, a nervous habit that suggested he was debating whether or not to share sensitive information. "I probably shouldn't be talking about this, but since Helen died and things have gotten worse..." He trailed off, then seemed to make a decision.

"Maya asks a lot of questions. Not medical questions about Mister Brennan's care, which would make sense, but questions about the family's business, their finances, their relationships. She wanted to know about Mister Brennan's investments, his property holdings, his legal arrangements."

I frowned. That sounded more than a little out of line. "And what did you tell her?"

"I don't know anything to tell," he replied. "I take care of the grounds, not the family's personal business. But Maya, she's also been going through Mister Brennan's papers when she thinks no one is looking. I've seen her in places she shouldn't be, at times when she should be focused on caregiving."

That was significant. "What kind of papers?" I asked.

"I've seen her in his study late at night, through the window, going through his desk, looking at documents that have nothing to do with his medical care. When I asked what she was doing, she said she was helping him organize his affairs because his memory wasn't reliable anymore."

"Did you believe her?"

"At first, maybe. It seemed reasonable enough that someone with his condition might need help organizing paperwork. But then I started paying closer attention to what she was actually doing."

Morrison led me to a workbench where he kept his gardening tools and notebooks. "I've made note, you see, Mister Starke," he said. "Dates, times, what I observed. Helen suggested I do it after she started getting suspicious."

"Helen Foster suggested you keep records?" I asked, surprised.

"About three weeks before she died. She came out here one evening, said she was worried about some things she'd noticed in the house. Asked if I'd seen anything unusual about Maya's behavior or if I'd noticed any changes in Mr. Brennan's condition."

Morrison retrieved a small notebook from beneath some seed catalogs. "Helen said if anything happened to her, I should give this to someone who could use it properly. She seemed genuinely worried about something, more worried than I'd ever seen her."

He handed me the notebook, and I saw it was filled with handwritten entries, organized chronologically, with detailed observations about Maya's activities around the Brennan estate. Each entry was dated and timed.

"March 15th - Maya in Mr. B's study at 11 PM, going through desk drawers. Said she was organizing papers when I asked."

"March 18th - Overheard Maya on phone in garden, talking to someone about 'timeline' and 'complications.' When she saw me, claimed it was her doctor about a medical appointment." And so on for at least a couple of weeks.

"This is some pretty detailed surveillance," I said.

He shrugged self-consciously. "Helen asked me to do it. She said she was worried Maya was taking advantage of Mister Brennan, but she needed evidence to prove it. She said her background made her naturally suspicious of people who seemed too good to be true, and Maya's behavior had triggering warning signs. I didn't understand what she meant by that."

"Her background?" I asked.

Morrison looked surprised, as if I should have known something obvious. "I'm surprised you don't know? Helen wasn't always a cook. She used to be a private investigator in Atlanta. Worked for some big firm there for years before she came to Chattanooga after her husband died."

So Helen had been conducting a professional-level investigation into Maya Santos, and she'd recruited Morrison to help her gather evidence using surveillance techniques she'd learned during her previous career.

"Did Helen tell you what she suspected Maya of doing?"

He thought for a moment, then said, "She thought Maya was drugging Mister Brennan to make him more compliant, and that she was planning to steal his money somehow. Helen said she'd seen this kind of thing before in Atlanta—caregivers who took advantage of elderly clients and drained them of their assets."

"What about you?" I asked. "Did you share Helen's suspicions?"

Morrison closed the notebook and looked toward the main house, his expression reflecting the internal conflict of someone who wanted to believe the best about people but couldn't ignore troubling evidence. "I didn't want to believe it at first. Maya seemed so devoted to Mister Brennan, so professional. But the more I watched, the more I realized Helen was right to be suspicious."

"About what specifically?" I asked.

"The pattern of Mister Brennan's confusion. It wasn't random like you'd expect with normal aging. It corresponded to when Maya gave him his medications. And Maya's interest in his financial affairs went way beyond what a caregiver should need to know."

Morrison opened another section of his notebook, revealing even more detailed observations. "I also made notes about something else Helen asked me to watch for. Maya's been receiving visitors that don't go through normal channels."

"What kind of visitors?" I asked.

"People who don't come to the front door or announce themselves properly. They meet her in the garden or by the garage, always when Mister Brennan is sleeping or when other family members aren't around. Very secretive meetings," he finished, leaning forward, conspiratorially.

He showed me more entries detailing these mysterious meetings, each one carefully documented with times, descriptions, and circumstances. "Same person, usually. Middle-aged woman, drives a silver sedan, license plate I couldn't see clearly. They usually talk for ten or fifteen minutes, then she leaves."

"How often?" I asked.

"Every couple of weeks or so," he replied. But more frequently this past month."

"Did Helen know about these meetings?"

"Oh yes. She was very interested when I told her, but she never said why."

"Mister Morrison, did Helen ever tell you she felt threatened or afraid?"

Morrison's expression grew somber, and he lowered his voice as if sharing a dangerous secret. "The last time I talked to her, about a week before she died, she seemed nervous. But what I asked her what was wrong, she said it was nothing, and that I should be careful."

"Hmm, I wonder what it was?" I muttered.

"Yeah, me too," Morrison said. "She never said, but she did ask me to search Maya's room if I ever got the chance. She said there might be something there that would prove what Maya was really up to."

I frowned. "She asked you to search Maya's room? Why would she do that? She worked inside the house. She could have done it herself."

"Uh, yes, she did, but she finished every day between two and three. Maya was always there when she was. She has a bedroom on the second floor of the main house, right next to Mr. Brennan's room."

I felt a surge of interest. "Were you able to search her room?"

Morrison nodded, looking around nervously. "See, I ain't normally allowed in the main house, being the groundskeeper, like. But last week—last Tuesday—when Maya went to town for groceries... It was just after four in the afternoon and I felt terrible about it, about going through someone's personal belongings, but Helen said it might be the only way to protect Mister Brennan."

"Did you find anything?" I asked, hopefully.

Morrison looked around nervously, then leaned in closer again and lowered his voice. "Medical journals. Textbooks about pharmacology and toxicology, herbalist magazines, stuff like that."

"Poisons?" I asked.

"I don't know nothing about that, but plant-based toxins, now that I do know about. Things that occur naturally and might not show up in routine blood tests. There were articles in them magazines about digitalis from foxglove, aconitine from monkshood, and something called ricin that comes from castor beans."

The discovery was troubling, but again circumstantial, and I tried to keep an open mind about possible innocent explanations. "Did you see anything else that might explain why she had these materials?"

He shook his head. "No, sir. I was going to tell Helen what I'd found, but she died before I got the chance. Since then, I've been carrying this information around, not knowing what to do with it."

"Mister Morrison, I wouldn't worry yourself about it. There could be innocent explanations. You have beautiful gardens here… Do you have foxglove and monkshood and the other thing here?"

"The castor beans, no. But foxglove and monkshood, yes, of course we do."

"Then maybe Maya was researching these topics for continuing education, or because she was concerned about Mr. Brennan's symptoms."

"You think she's trying to help him, then?" he asked skeptically.

"I don't know what to think yet. But yes, it's possible. The materials are concerning, but if it wasn't her, and she thought it might be someone else—"

"What? Lisa and Mark?" he snapped, interrupting me. "Not a chance. I watched them kids grow up… Well, not actually grow up, but you know I mean. They love that old man. Wouldn't harm a hair on his head."

"I'm sure you're right," I said, trying to ease his mind. But we need more evidence before we can draw conclusions about her intentions."

But Morrison's face remained troubled. It was the expression of someone who'd seen too much to have his concerns dismissed so easily. "Mister Starke, there's something else. Something I found in Maya's room I didn't understand, not at first."

"What was that?"

"A collection of newspaper obituaries. All elderly people, all from cities where Maya used to work, according to what I'd heard. And next to each obituary, she'd written dollar amounts in red ink."

"Dollar amounts?" I asked frowning.

"Fifty thousand, seventy-five thousand, one hundred thousand. Different amounts for different people. I don't know what it means, but it seemed strange for a caregiver to be collecting obituaries and making notes about money."

This was more concerning, though again I had to consider alternative explanations. "She might have been keeping track of bequests from former clients, or maybe documenting cases for some kind of research or legal purpose."

"Maybe," Morrison said, though he didn't sound convinced. "But why would she need that information if she's just providing medical care?"

"You need to be careful, Mister Morrison. If Maya is genuinely caring for Mister Brennan, innocent, we don't want to violate her privacy unnecessarily. But if she's not…" I trailed off, not wanting to lead this simple man into imagining things that as yet we couldn't prove. And by simple, I don't mean he was simple-minded, just that he led a simple life.

"And if she's not?" he said, pushing me.

"Then we need to think again," I replied. "We need

to be cautious until we understand what we're really dealing with."

As we walked back toward the main house, I thought about what Morrison had uncovered. The materials in Maya's room were suspicious, but they weren't definitive proof of criminal intent. There could be an innocent explanation for her research into toxicology and her collection of obituaries, though the pattern was certainly troubling.

Helen Foster had died trying to uncover the truth about what was happening to Walker Brennan—if anything—and her investigation had involved James Morrison and his careful documentation. What he'd found was concerning, but not convincing, to a jury, at least. To me? Yes, I was slowly getting there. Maya Santos certainly looked guilty based on the circumstantial evidence, but looking guilty and being guilty weren't necessarily the same thing.

Either way, Morrison's revelations had given our investigation a new direction and even urgency, even if we didn't yet have definitive answers about Maya Santos's true intentions regarding Walter Brennan.

10

MEDICAL MYSTERY

AFTER LEAVING JAMES MORRISON WITH INSTRUCTIONS to document any further suspicious activities and to contact me immediately if anything unusual occurred, I drove directly to Dr. Walker's medical practice. The evidence Morrison had found in Maya's room was troubling enough to warrant immediate professional consultation, but I needed expert medical opinion about Walter Brennan's symptoms and the possibility that he was being systematically poisoned with sophisticated compounds.

Dr. Walker's office was busy with the usual stream of elderly patients that filled most geriatric practices in the late afternoon. The waiting room was crowded with people dealing with the various ailments that came with advanced age, and the atmosphere carried the familiar medicinal smell of a facility that specialized in complex chronic conditions. I waited nearly an hour before she could see me, using the time to review my notes about Walter's documented symptoms and the timeline of his decline that Morrison had so carefully recorded.

"Mister Starke," Walker said as I entered her office, her professional demeanor immediately apparent, "I wasn't expecting to see you again so soon. Has there been a change in Walter's condition?"

"That's what I'm hoping you can help me determine. His family is still concerned about his claims that he's being poisoned, and we've uncovered something that makes those claims seem more credible than we initially thought."

Dr. Walker's expression remained professionally neutral, but I caught a slight tightening around her eyes that suggested the conversation was moving into territory that made her uncomfortable. "What have you found?" she asked.

I dodged the question by asking another. "What do you know about plant-based toxins, Doctor?" I asked, then followed it with another question. "Could he have ingested something like that that might account for his deteriorating condition?"

She shook her head. "Mister Starke, I've examined Walter thoroughly on multiple occasions. His symptoms are consistent with normal aging, combined with anxiety and paranoid ideation. I've seen no clinical evidence of poisoning of any kind."

"But you haven't specifically tested for exotic toxins, have you?"

Dr. Walker leaned back in her chair, her demeanor becoming more defensive as the conversation moved toward challenging her medical judgment. "Standard toxicology screening covers the most common substances that people encounter. Testing for exotic plant toxins or unusual pharmaceutical compounds requires specific knowledge of what to look for and can be extremely expensive."

"What if I could provide that specific knowledge, Doctor?"

"What exactly are you suggesting, Mister Starke?"

I decided to be direct rather than dance around the implications. "I'm suggesting that Walter Brennan may be the victim of a carefully planned poisoning, and that his symptoms warrant comprehensive toxicological analysis to determine if he's being given substances that wouldn't show up on routine tests."

Dr. Walker stood up and walked to the window, apparently considering my request while looking out at the parking lot. When she turned back, her expression was troubled in a way that suggested she was taking the possibility seriously. "Mister Starke, if you're serious about this, if you really believe Walter is being deliberately poisoned, then we need to approach this carefully. Some toxins are incredibly difficult to detect, and the testing process itself can be complicated and expensive."

"Walter's family is prepared to pay for whatever testing is necessary."

"It's not just about money," she replied, "though that's certainly a factor. If someone is sophisticated enough to use exotic toxins, they've probably chosen substances that metabolize quickly or mimic natural disease processes. We might need to catch them in the act, so to speak."

"And how would we do that?" I asked, frowning and wondering why the hell she was balking at a tox screen.

Dr. Walker returned to her desk, turned to the bookshelf behind it, took out a medical reference book, and flipped through pages that appeared to be well-marked with notes and bookmarks. "Many plant-based toxins, for example, cause symptoms that are identical to heart problems, neurological disorders, or gastrointestinal illnesses. Unless you test for the specific compound within hours of exposure, the evidence disappears from the bloodstream."

"So Walter's saved food and medication samples are worthless, then?" I said.

"It depends on how they were stored and how long ago the contamination occurred. Mister Starke, there's something else you need to understand. If Walter is being poisoned with some sophisticated compound, whoever's doing it has significant medical knowledge."

"Do tell," I said, wrinkling my brow even further.

She blinked, tilted her head, then said, "Understanding of pharmacokinetics, metabolism, drug interactions, dosage calculations. This isn't someone putting rat poison in his coffee. This would be someone who understands how to cause specific symptoms while avoiding detection by standard medical examinations."

The implication was chilling. If Walter was being systematically poisoned, his attacker had medical expertise that went beyond what a typical caregiver would possess, suggesting either advanced training or extensive research.

"So what specific tests could we run, then?"

She opened the reference book again, then closed it and said, "I suppose we could test for cardiac glycosides like digitalis or oleander compounds. These cause heart rhythm abnormalities and can be lethal if ingested over time, especially in elderly patients with existing cardiac issues."

"What about other plant toxins?"

"Aconitine from monkshood or wolfsbane plants. It's extremely toxic and can cause the kind of weakness and confusion Walter has been experiencing. Various alkaloids from the nightshade family of plants that affect the nervous system."

Dr. Walker made notes as she spoke. "The problem is that each test is specific and expensive. We'd need to know which compounds to look for, or we'd have to run a comprehensive panel that could cost thousands of dollars and still miss something."

"So how would we decide which tests to run?" I asked, becoming more frustrated by the minute.

"By analyzing Walter's specific symptoms and their progression over time. If someone has been poisoning him systematically, there should be a pattern that corresponds to particular types of toxins."

I shook my head, but said nothing.

Dr. Walker went to a file cabinet, extracted a file, and opened it on her desk. It was Brennan's file, the accumulated documentation of months of medical care. "Let me review his symptom progression and see if I can identify any patterns that might suggest specific compounds."

She studied the file for several minutes, making notes and occasionally referring to her reference books. Her expression grew increasingly concerned as she reviewed the timeline of Walter's decline. "Walter's symptoms have included weakness, dizziness, nausea, confusion, and cardiac irregularities. The progression has been gradual over several months."

"And that suggests a particular type of toxin?" I asked.

"It could," she replied, cautiously. "Perhaps something that accumulates in the system or causes cumulative damage. Cardiac glycosides would fit that pattern, as would certain heavy metals or alkaloid compounds that build up in tissue over time."

"Would these substances be detectable in blood tests now?"

Dr. Walker appeared to consider the question carefully. "Possibly, if the exposure has been recent and if we test for the right compounds. But Mister Starke, there's something else we need to consider."

"What's that?" I asked.

"If Walter is being poisoned, and if we start running comprehensive toxicology tests, whoever is doing it will know we're onto them. They might speed up their timeline or eliminate the evidence."

"Or eliminate him," I muttered.

"Exactly. We need to be very careful about how we proceed with any testing regimen."

I thought about the delicate balance we faced.

Walter needed immediate medical evaluation to determine if he was being poisoned, but investigating his condition might put him in greater danger if his attacker realized they were being exposed.

"Doctor Walker, what if we approached this differently? What if we hospitalized Walter for observation and testing, claiming he was having cardiac episodes or neurological problems?"

"That might work," she said. "If we admitted him for a comprehensive evaluation of his existing symptoms, we could run the toxicology tests as part of a broader medical workup without raising suspicion."

"And that would give us the evidence we need?" I asked.

"It would give us definitive answers about whether or not he's being poisoned. But Mister Starke, if the tests come back positive, if we prove Walter is being deliberately poisoned, that makes this a criminal matter."

No shit, I thought. "I understand," said. "But if someone is trying to kill him, we need proof that will hold up in court."

She made more notes in Walter's file, her pen moving quickly across the pages. "All right. I can arrange for Walter to be admitted to Memorial Hospital tomorrow morning. We'll tell his family and his caregiver that he's been having concerning symptoms that require immediate evaluation. Cardiac arrhythmias, possible mini-strokes, medication interactions. All legitimate concerns given his age and medical history, and all requiring the kind of comprehensive testing that would reveal toxic compounds."

She closed Walter's file and looked at me seriously. "Mr. Starke, I have to ask: do you have a specific suspect in mind?"

I hesitated, unsure how much to reveal about our investigation. "Let's say I have concerns and leave it at that. Is there anything else we should be looking for?"

She took a prescription pad from her desk drawer and began writing. "I'm going to order some preliminary blood work that we can do before the hospitalization. Basic chemistry panel, cardiac enzymes, and a few specific tests for compounds that might explain his symptoms."

"How long will that take?" I asked.

"Twenty-four hours for most tests, forty-eight for the more specialized ones. But Mr. Starke, I want you to understand something; if these tests come back positive, if we prove Walter is being systematically poisoned, his life is in immediate danger."

"I know that, Doctor," I replied, a little more sharply than I probably should have.

The implications were sobering. Our investigation might save Walter's life by proving he was being poisoned, but it might also have the opposite effect, and thus cause his immediate demise.

"Doctor Walker, when you admit Walter to the hospital tomorrow, can you make sure no unauthorized people have access to his room or his medications?"

"Absolutely. Hospital security protocols are much

stricter than home care. No one without proper medical credentials will be able to access Walter or administer any substances to him."

What about his primary caregiver? I wondered, but I kept the thought to myself.

She handed me the prescription for Walter's preliminary blood work. "Mister Starke, I want you to coordinate this with local law enforcement. If we're dealing with attempted murder, the police need to be involved from the beginning."

"I'm already working with Captain Kate Gazzara," I replied.

"Good. Have her contact me directly so we can coordinate the medical and legal aspects of this investigation."

As I prepared to leave Dr. Walker's office, I had a thought: "Doctor Walker, one more question. In your experience, how common is this type of systematic poisoning?"

"More common than most people realize, unfortunately. Elder abuse involving poisoning or medication manipulation happens more often than it's detected, partly because the symptoms mimic natural aging processes."

"And the perpetrators?" I asked.

"Usually people with medical knowledge or training. Nurses, caregivers, sometimes family members with access to medical information. In this case, if what you say is true, the sophistication required to pull off this kind of poisoning suggests someone with significant pharmaceutical knowledge."

Dr. Walker's assessment confirmed my suspicions about Maya Santos while also raising troubling questions about the scope of the potential crime. If Maya had the medical knowledge to systematically poison Walter Brennan using powerful exotic toxins, she might also have used similar methods on her previous clients.

As I left the medical building, I called Kate to update her on the plan to hospitalize Walter. We were finally going to get definitive answers about whether Walter Brennan was being poisoned, but those answers might come at a cost; his accelerated demise.

The next twenty-four hours would determine whether our investigation saved Walter's life or inadvertently triggered his murder. Either way, we'd discover the truth about what was happening in the Brennan household, and whether Maya Santos was a devoted caregiver or a sophisticated killer who'd perfected the art of undetectable murder.

11

THE SECOND DEATH

It was nine o'clock the next morning, Saturday, when the phone rang. I was having breakfast at home with Amanda and Jade and the early morning call immediately set me on edge. In my line of work, early morning weekend phone calls rarely brought good news. Kate's name appeared on the display, and something in the early hour of the call made me immediately apprehensive about what she might have discovered.

"Harry, we've got another body. James Morrison, the groundskeeper from the Brennan estate. He was found dead in the greenhouse about an hour ago."

I felt ice in my stomach as the implications hit me. "Do we know what happened?" I asked.

"It looks like an accidental exposure to pesticides. But given your investigation and the timing, I thought you'd want to know right away."

I glanced at Amanda, took a deep breath, then said, "Okay, I'll be right there." And I ended the call.

Amanda looked up from helping Jade with her cereal, her expression one of concern. It was many years before I fully understood that came from years of being married to someone whose life was often in jeopardy. "Work?" she asked, quietly.

"Yep," I replied. "Sorry, it could be a long day."

"Be careful," she said, and I could see the worry in her eyes. She'd learned to read the signs and could tell when a case was turning dangerous, and the tension in my voice had clearly triggered her protective instincts.

"It's okay," I said. "It's just another body in an already complicated case."

She nodded. I drank the rest of my coffee, stood up, slipped into my shoulder rig and suit jacket, kissed them both and made my exit without saying another word except, "I'll call you."

I ARRIVED at the Brennan estate some thirty minutes later to find it bustling with police activity. The greenhouse was surrounded with crime scene tape, and I could see Kate standing just inside the tape, feet apart, fists on her hips, talking to two CSI techs. Multiple patrol cars lined the driveway, their flashing lights creating an atmosphere of urgency and danger. Samson sat near her car, alert but calm, his presence a reassuring constant in what was shaping up to be a very bad morning.

"Hey, buddy," I said as I approached.

He looked up at me and I swear he winked at me. I reached down and scratched the fur behind his ears.

"Harry," Kate said as she ducked under the tape.

"Hey, Kate," I said. "You look…"

"Don't even go there," she said. "It's been a rough morning."

"I bet," I replied. "So the groundskeeper is dead, huh? I could almost it figures. I was talking to him yesterday afternoon. What do we know?"

She bit her bottom lip and slowly shook her head before answering. "Morrison was found dead in the greenhouse by Maya Santos about an hour ago. She called 911 immediately, very distraught, according to the responding officers. Come on, you can take a look"

Kate led me toward the greenhouse with Samson beside us. He didn't seem concerned, and I took that as a good sign.

"Morrison was apparently working with some kind of fumigation system when something went wrong. The greenhouse was full of toxic fumes when Maya found him."

"What kind of fumigation?" I asked.

"Phosphine gas, according to the equipment we found. It's used to kill insects and rodents, but it's extremely dangerous in enclosed spaces without proper ventilation. Even experienced exterminators have died from exposure to it."

We stopped outside the greenhouse, where I could see Morrison's body still in place some thirty feet away, with Doc Sheddon standing just to the rear of the body, head down, making notes. Even from a distance, it was clear he'd died in distress. He was face down, arms outstretched, his body positioned in a way that suggested he'd been trying to reach the door when he was overcome.

"Kate, the timing; it can't be a coincidence," I said as I stood with hands in my pants pockets, staring down the interior of the greenhouse at the body. "He was helping Helen Foster investigate Maya Santos, and now he's dead less than twelve hours after he talked to me."

"I know," she replied. "That's why I called you immediately instead of waiting for the standard notification process."

"How did you know?" I asked, frowning. I'd told nobody.

"Maya told me. She saw you from the window."

"Hah!" I said. "What's her story?"

"She says she came out to the greenhouse at about eight to ask Morrison about some garden maintenance for Mr. Brennan's upcoming birthday celebration. She found the door closed and could smell something chemical. When she opened the door, she saw Morrison on the floor and immediately called for help."

"Did she try to help him?" I asked.

"She says she was afraid to go into the greenhouse because of the fumes," Kate replied. "Which was a smart decision, actually. If she'd gone in without protective equipment, we might have two bodies instead of one."

From the doorway, I studied the greenhouse, noting the ventilation system and the fumigation equipment that was still in place. The greenhouse vents were all closed, which I thought was unusual, but what do I know? The setup looked professional but complex, the kind of system that required knowledge and experience to operate safely.

"Kate," I said, "Morrison has been working with this equipment for twenty years. Would he make a mistake that would kill him?"

"That's what we need to figure out," she replied. "But Harry, there's something else you need to know."

"What?" I asked.

"Morrison's apartment above the garage was broken into sometime last night. Maya discovered it this morning. She said the door was open, and it looked like the place had been ransacked."

I slowly shook my head. *Was it Maya who broke in to make it look like it was something it wasn't? Or was it someone else?* The implications were troubling.

"There's no point in asking if anything was missing, I suppose?" I asked.

She shook her. "No. but I've asked Mike to process it. Maya says she didn't go inside because she was afraid whoever had broken in might still be there."

Kate gestured toward the garage building, where I could see more police cars there, too."

"The notebook Morrison showed me yesterday had a lot of detailed notes about suspicious activities. If someone wanted to…"

"They might have killed Morrison to get it," she finished for me.

Doc Seddon approached us, waddling slowly along

the center of the greenhouse, pulling off his latex gloves and looking grim.

"Harry, my boy," he said, stuffing the gloves in his pocket. "I'm surprised to see you here. What's the haps? Hello, Sammy." He bent down and patted the dog's head.

I nodded toward the body. "Jim Morrison," I said. "What's the verdict?"

He looked around, back the way he'd came, then turned to face us, sighed and shook his head. "Ut's a nasty one. My preliminary examination suggests death by phosphine poisoning. It has all the classic symptoms. There would have been chronic respiratory distress followed by cardiac arrest, and he would also have suffered neurological effects. He died in agony, poor chap. It's a very unpleasant way to die."

"Any idea of the time of death?" I asked.

He looked at me over his spectacles and said, "Sometime between seven and eight this morning. The body was still warm when I arrived.

"How long would it have taken for him to die?" I asked.

"In a confined space like this one with a high concentration?" He paused, made a face, then said, "Ten, maybe as much as fifteen minutes of intense suffering. The victim would have been conscious and aware for most of it."

"Could it have been accidental?" Kate asked.

Doc considered the question for a moment, then said, "It's possible, but the circumstances are unusual. Morrison was an experienced horticulturist, and the safety protocols for phosphine fumigation are well-established in the industry."

Kate made notes as Doc Sheddon spoke. "What about the equipment? Any signs of malfunction?" she asked.

"The ventilation system appears to have malfunctioned," he replied. "The top vents are all closed and some of the fans aren't working properly, which means, if I'm right, that the air wasn't circulating which would have allowed gas to accumulate to dangerous levels."

I felt a chill in by bones. "Doc, it all sounds a little simple. Someone, knowing he was about to fumigate the greenhouse, could easily have closed the vents and tampered with the fans and the equipment."

He nodded. "It's possible, but we'd need a thorough technical analysis to determine if the failures were accidental or intentional. The manufacturer will need to examine the equipment."

I stared at him for a moment, then nodded. "Thanks, Doc. You've been helpful, as always."

"I'll have them remove the body," he replied. "I'll do the post tomorrow morning. I'll call you, Kate, if I find anything. You both know where I am if you need me." And with that, he grabbed up his bag and walked slowly away to his SUV.

Kate and I watched him go, then walked around the exterior of the greenhouse, examining the ventilation system. The vents were electrically operated automatically, as were the fans and the rest of the equipment. The system looked complex enough that tampering with it would require some technical knowledge, but not necessarily advanced training.

"Harry, if someone sabotaged the system to kill Morrison, they'd need to understand how it works and they'd need to have access to the greenhouse."

"Maya Santos has been working at this estate for months. She'd know Morrison's routine, and she'd have access to all areas of the property."

"But would she have the technical knowledge to sabotage ventilation equipment?"

That was a good question. Maya's background was in caregiving, not mechanical systems.

We were interrupted by one of the CSI techs processing Morrison's apartment. "Captain Gazzara, you need to see this."

We climbed the external stairs to Morrison's apartment above the garage, where the search had revealed the extent of the break-in. Furniture had been moved, drawers had been emptied, and personal papers were scattered across the floor in what appeared to be a systematic search.

"Whoever did this was looking for something specific," the tech said. "They went through everything, but they took nothing of value that we know of. The television, laptop computer, jewelry; it's all still here."

"Do you have any idea what they might have been looking for?" Kate asked.

"It's hard to say," she replied. "The place is pretty torn up. But we did find this."

The officer handed Kate a small notebook that had been hidden under a loose floorboard, which was in turn hidden under the carpet. It was the same one Morrison had shown me the day before.

"So they missed it," I said.

"Either that or they weren't looking for it," Kate replied. "They might have been looking for something else. What if Morrison made copies, or if he'd shared them with other people...?"

"Then this might not be the only record of what he'd discovered," I muttered, thoughtfully. "May I...?" I asked, holding out my hand.

She handed it to me and I flipped through the notebook, reading his detailed observations about late-night activities, mysterious visitors, and concerning patterns of behavior. The information was potentially damaging to someone who was trying to operate without scrutiny, but was it enough to justify murder?

"Kate, it contains observations that could be embarrassing, maybe even incriminating, to someone. But I'm not sure it's enough to justify murder."

"Unless Morrison knew more than he wrote down," she replied. "Maybe he witnessed something specific that made him a direct threat."

That was possible. Morrison had been nosing around for weeks, and he might have seen something that went beyond what he'd documented in his notebook, something that could expose a killer's identity or methods.

My phone rang. It was Dr. Walker. "Mr. Starke," she said when I answered, "I've been trying to reach Walter about his hospital admission, but Maya says he's having a very difficult morning and can't come to the phone. She seems quite upset about something."

"Doctor Walker, James Morrison was found dead this morning. Given the timing and our concerns about Walter's safety, I think we need to get him to the hospital immediately."

"Oh my God. Another death? Oh dear, oh dear. Yes, I agree we need to get Walter to safety immediately. I'll arrange for an ambulance to transport him for emergency evaluation."

"What reason will you give?" I asked.

"Cardiac concerns based on his recent symptoms and the stress of recent events, that would be completely legitimate given his age and medical history."

"Can Maya stop him from being hospitalized?" I asked.

"Not if I order it as his physician," she replied. "She may object, but she can't legally interfere with necessary medical care."

After I hung up, Kate looked at me with concern. "Harry, if someone killed Morrison to protect themselves, taking Walter away from the house might force them to make a desperate move."

"And it might just save his life, Kate. Two people connected to this household are now dead under suspicious circumstances. Walter could be next if we don't act quickly."

"But we still don't have definitive proof these deaths are connected," she replied, "or that anyone is deliberately targeting people around the Brennan family."

Kate was right to be cautious. She was, is, after all, a cop, and cops need probable cause; I didn't, and the pattern was becoming difficult to ignore. Helen Foster dies of a heart attack just as she's investigating suspicious activities. James Morrison dies in an equipment accident shortly after sharing his observations with me. Both deaths appeared natural or accidental, but both eliminated potential witnesses to whatever was happening at the Brennan estate.

"Kate, can you put a protective detail on Walter once he's hospitalized?" I asked. "We need to monitor his visitors, if any."

"Including Maya Santos?" she asked, smiling.

"Especially Maya Santos," I replied. "She's either the most unlucky caregiver in history, or she's connected to these deaths in ways we don't understand yet."

"I'll see what I can do," she replied. "In the meantime, I'll continue the investigation into the two deaths."

"Yeah, you do that," I said, "but keep an open mind about whether Morrison's death really was accidental. I don't think it was. The timing is too convenient, and the circumstances are too suspicious."

She nodded. "And if we determine it was murder—?"

"Then we'll have our first piece of concrete evidence that someone is willing to kill to protect whoever it is that's targeting Walter Brennan," I said, interrupting her.

As I left the Brennan estate, I couldn't shake the feeling that Morrison's death had escalated the situation beyond simple elder abuse or financial fraud. If someone was systematically eliminating witnesses and potential threats, then Walter Brennan was indeed in immediate danger, and anyone and everyone investigating the case could be at risk as well.

The question had now become whether the two deaths were the work of Maya Santos, as the evidence seemed to suggest, or whether someone else was orchestrating the events to make Maya appear guilty. Me? I didn't like that idea.

12

SUSPICIOUS ALIBIS

KATE'S INVESTIGATION INTO MORRISON'S DEATH BEGAN immediately, and within hours, it became clear that everyone connected to the Brennan household had questionable alibis for the time when the groundskeeper died. What should have been a straightforward process of elimination instead revealed a web of suspicious behavior that made the case more complicated rather than clearer. The lack of solid alibis was almost too convenient, as if everyone involved had deliberately arranged to be unaccounted for during the critical time period.

I met Kate at the police department that afternoon. She was in her office coordinating interviews with the potential suspects. The incident room itself buzzed with activity as officers processed evidence and compiled witness statements. Samson lay beside her desk, occasionally lifting his head when someone new entered her office. Kate had spread out a detailed timeline on her desk, marking the estimated time of Morrison's death and the claimed whereabouts of everyone who'd had access to the Brennan estate.

"This is turning into a nightmare," Kate said, pointing to her notes with frustration. "Nobody has a solid alibi, and everyone's story has holes you could drive a truck through."

"Why don't you start with Maya Santos?" I suggested.

"Santos claims she was in her room sleeping until around six-fifteen, when she got up to start her morning routine. Says she went to the kitchen first, then, sometime before eight, she decided to go check with Morrison about some garden work that needed doing that Mr. Brennan had mentioned the previous evening. She went to the greenhouse and found the place filled with what looked like white smoke."

"Has anyone verified that?" I asked.

"That's the problem. Walter was still asleep, according to Maya, and there are no other household staff who would have seen her during those critical early morning hours. She could have been anywhere on the property between, say, seven and eight when she says she 'discovered' the body."

Kate flipped to another page of notes, obviously frustrated. "But here's what's interesting; Maya's story is almost too detailed. She remembers exactly what she was thinking about when she woke up, what she had planned for breakfast, and why she decided to talk to Morrison about the garden work."

"And you think it was over-rehearsed?" I said.

"I don't now… Maybe," she replied. "Or maybe she's

just the kind of person who remembers details. I mean, she's a trained and experienced caregiver, so she could be expected to know what she needs to do at any given moment. Either way, we can't prove she was where she claims to be during the critical time period."

"What about the equipment?" I asked. "Is there any forensic evidence to suggest it was sabotaged?"

She shook her head and sighed. "The ventilation system definitely malfunctioned, but determining whether it was sabotage or mechanical failure is going to take time. The manufacturer is sending a technician to examine the equipment, but we won't have the results for several days."

Kate moved to the next section of her timeline. "Lisa Brennan is almost as problematic. She claims she was at her art gallery from about seven-thirty, trying to get some work done before the business day started."

"That early?" I asked, frowning.

"She says she couldn't sleep because of stress about her financial situation and her father's condition, so she decided to go to the gallery and work on her inventory and try to figure out what she could sell to raise money quickly."

"Did anyone see her there?" I asked.

"No. The gallery is downtown in a building that's mostly empty at that hour. No security cameras in the immediate area, no witnesses who can confirm she was there during the time Morrison died."

Kate showed me Lisa's statement, highlighting the specific details that seemed almost too convenient. "Like Maya, her story is very detailed. She remembers which pieces she was cataloging, what she was thinking about while she worked, and why she chose that particular morning to go in early."

"Sounds like another over-rehearsed alibi," I said. "Then again..." I trailed off.

"Or another person under extreme stress who's hyper-aware of details because everything in her life is falling apart. People do react differently to pressure, don't they?"

I nodded thoughtfully as I studied Kate's timeline, noting how the lack of solid alibis actually made the case more difficult rather than easier. With everyone unaccounted for, we couldn't eliminate any of them as suspects. "What about Mark Brennan?" I asked.

"Mark claims he was at home in his apartment, but that's where his story gets really problematic. He says he was awake most of the night because he's been having trouble sleeping due to his financial problems and the threats from Torrino's people."

I would have laughed had not Mark's situation been so dire. Instead, I said, "Insomnia isn't unusual for someone in his situation."

"No, but his neighbors didn't see his car in the parking lot when they left for work around seven-thirty. Mark claims he went for a drive around five-thirty because he was restless and couldn't stay in the apartment."

Kate took out another set of notes, stared at it for a moment, then said, "Mark says he drove around randomly for about an hour, maybe hour and a half, that he didn't go anywhere specific, didn't stop anywhere, didn't talk to anyone. Just drove around trying to clear his head."

"Understandable," I said.

"Right. And here's what makes it worse; Mark's apartment is only about fifteen minutes from the Brennan estate. He could easily have driven there, sabotaged the greenhouse equipment, and been back home before anyone missed him."

"But did he know Morrison's routine?" I asked. "And he could have known that he, Morrison, was going to be fumigating the greenhouse this morning?"

"He grew up on that estate. He'd know exactly when Morrison typically started work, where he'd be, and how to access the greenhouse without being seen by the main house. As to his intent to fumigate the place…" She shrugged. "Only Morrison could have told him that."

Kate's phone rang, and she answered it while continuing to review her notes. After a brief conversation, she hung up and looked at me with increased frustration.

"That was Corbin. He's interviewing Ruth Webb. Apparently, her alibi is just as problematic as everyone else's."

"But she wasn't working today, wasn't she?"

"No, she works Mondays and Thursdays. She was home until after ten this morning when she went to Publix for groceries. Her daughter was at a sleepover. She keeps her car in the garage, out of sight."

"So she has no alibi for this morning when Morrison died?" I said.

"Right. And like everyone else, she knows the Brennan estate well enough to access the greenhouse without being detected."

I leaned back in my chair and closed my eyes for a moment, then said, "It's a puzzlement, isn't it? It has to be one of them... My money's still on Maya Santos. She's the only one with a viable motive. Lisa and Mark have nothing to gain from these two deaths, or from the death of Walter Brennan. Maya does. Eighty million bucks, and the deaths of Helen and Morrison eliminate a couple noseys that were digging into her activities. We should concentrate on her."

Kate shook her head. "Walter hasn't yet signed his will, remember? That provides both Lisa and Mark with motive either individually or together. And any of them could have known what Morrison's schedule was. All they had to do was ask him. And they could have researched the fumigation system online, and the sabotage couldn't have been particularly sophisticated; disconnect some power cables, so the vents don't open and... I dunno. It can't be that difficult, can it?"

"Probably not," I replied. "Which means we're back to motive and opportunity, and everyone qualifies."

"Unfortunately, yes. Everyone had reason to want Morrison silenced, and everyone had the opportunity to do it."

Kate's phone rang again, answered it, listened for a moment, then frowned and said, "We'll be right there," she said, hanging up quickly.

"What's up?"

"That was Memorial Hospital," she said, gathering

up her things. "Walter Brennan was admitted this morning as planned, but there's been a complication."

"What kind of complication?"

"Someone tried to visit him who wasn't on the approved list. When security questioned them, they turned away and left immediately without providing identification."

I felt a chill run through me. "Did they get a description?" I asked.

"Middle-aged woman, average height, dark hair. Could match Maya, Lisa or Ruth, but the security camera footage might give us more details."

"When did this happen?" I asked.

"About an hour ago," she replied. "Hospital security has increased Walter's protection, but whoever tried to see him now knows he's there and under guard."

"Harry," she said, "if someone killed Morrison to eliminate him as a witness, they might be desperate enough to try something at the hospital."

I didn't need to answer that one.

"And it means our killer is getting reckless. Trying to access Walter at the hospital was a big risk."

"Come on, Harry," Kate said as she gathered her files and headed for the door, Samson at her heels. "We need to go and review the hospital security footage. Maybe we can identify this mysterious visitor."

The lack of solid alibis should have helped us narrow our suspect list, but instead it confirmed that principal players had both the motive and opportunity to kill James Morrison and Helen Foster.

The attempt to visit Walter at the hospital suggested

that our killer was becoming desperate, willing to take increasingly dangerous risks. But it also suggested they were making mistakes, becoming less careful as the pressure mounted.

"Kate," I said as we drove toward the hospital, "whoever tried to visit Walter today made a critical error. They exposed themselves to hospital security when they could have just waited."

"Unless waiting wasn't an option," she replied. "If the killer's timeline has been accelerated by Morrison's death and Walter's hospitalization, they might feel like they're running out of opportunities."

Samson's head appeared between our seats. I ruffled his ears and said, "What do you think, boy?" He just looked at me, panting gently, he togue lolling out. Then he he licked his lips, snapped his jaws closed and backed away onto the rear seat.

"Yeah," I said. "Me, too, buddy."

13

THE HELPER'S PAST

HEATHER CALLED ME WHILE KATE AND I WERE ON OUR way to the hospital and she sounded excited.

"Harry, I've had Corbin following Ruth Webb like you asked, and, well, we need to talk."

"Go on," I said. "What did you find?"

"Ruth Webb isn't who she claims to be."

"Where are you?"

"I'm at the Coffee Shop on Market Street."

I looked at Kate, who was listening to my side of the conversation while navigating the afternoon traffic.

"Go," she said without hesitation. "I can handle the hospital security review. If Heather's found something, we need to know about it."

"Okay," I replied, thinking. "If you'll drop me off at Market Street."

"Of course. And, Harry, stay in touch. If Heather's discovered something important, I need to know."

Kate changed direction and headed toward downtown.

"Keep me posted on the security footage," I said. "And Kate, be careful. If someone tried to visit Walter today, they might still be in the hospital watching."

The Coffee Shop was one of those generic chains that was the same if you were in Chattanooga or Chicago, the kind of place where conversations could blend into the background noise and surveillance work could be conducted without attracting attention. Heather was seated in a corner booth with her laptop open and several manila folders spread across the table.

"Harry, sit down. This is going to take a few minutes to explain properly," she said, looking up at me.

I nodded, ordered coffee, and then joined Heather at her table.

"Start from the beginning," I said. "What have you found?"

"I've been following Ruth Webb for the past two days, documenting her routine, her contacts, and her activities. What I found is that Ruth has been lying about almost everything, starting with her identity."

Heather opened the first folder and showed me a collection of documents and photographs that immediately caught my attention. Birth certificates, employment records, and family photographs that painted a picture that differed completely from what we'd been told.

"Ruth Webb's real name is Ruth Clemens. She's Helen Foster's niece."

Now that, I have to admit, took me by surprise. I stared at her. "No kidding? Helen Foster's niece?"

"Helen Foster never married, never had children. But she did have a sister, Sarah, who Married Anthony Clemens and had a daughter named Ruth. Sarah died ten years ago in a car accident, and Ruth took her step-father's last name, Webb, when her mother remarried briefly before Sarah's death."

"Go on," I said.

"Apparently, Ruth has been in regular contact with her aunt Helen for years. They were close. Helen helped Ruth financially when she was struggling as a single mother, provided emotional support, and considered Ruth more like a daughter than a niece."

Heather showed me phone records and email communications between Helen and Ruth that revealed the depth of their relationship. "They talked at least twice a week, and Helen was mentoring Ruth, giving her advice about everything from finances to child-rearing to career decisions."

"But why would Ruth take a cleaning job at the Brennan house?" I asked.

"That's where it gets interesting. Ruth didn't get the job through normal channels. Helen recommended her directly to Walter Brennan about six months ago, right around the time Maya Santos was hired as his caregiver."

I studied the timeline Heather had constructed. "So Helen arranged for Ruth to work at the Brennan house at the same time Maya arrived," I said, thoughtfully.

"It looks that way," Heather replied. "And based on the communications I found, Helen was already suspicious of Maya when she made the recommendation.

She wanted someone she trusted inside the household."

"So Hellen was setting up surveillance," I said. "It makes sense; a cleaner can go where a cook can't."

"Exactly. Ruth was reporting back to Helen about everything she observed. Maya's behavior, Walter's condition, changes in his routine, anything that seemed unusual or suspicious."

Heather opened another folder filled with printed emails and text messages. "Tim was able to recover some of the communications between Helen and Ruth from Ruth's phone backup files in the cloud. Helen was conducting a systematic investigation into Maya Santos, and Ruth was helping her. And Ruth was good at it. She has a background that made her a particularly valuable asset."

"What kind of background?" I asked.

"She worked as a pharmacy technician at Erlanger for three years before her daughter was born. She's well versed in medications, drug interactions, and pharmaceutical procedures. She understands how medications work and how they can be misused. She'd understand dosages, interactions, side effects, and how different drugs could be combined to cause specific symptoms. She'd be able to figure it out if someone was systematically poisoning Walter Brennan. She'd recognize the signs better than most."

Heather showed me Ruth's employment records and professional certifications. It was clear that she was no cleaning lady.

"Ruth left the Erlanger pharmacy when her

daughter was born because she's a single mother and the hours were difficult. She's since been working part time at CVS. And get this. It's important; she's also been doing some consulting work for Masterson Investigations in Atlanta."

"That is interesting," I said. "Masterson Investigations? Helen's former employer?"

"Yep, Ruth has been doing background checks and research for them on a freelance basis. She's not licensed as a private investigator, but she has the computer skills and knowledge, especially when it involves pharmaceutical issues.

The picture was becoming clearer, and it was far more complex than we'd imagined. Ruth was actively pursuing leads. She was trying to expose whatever was happening at the Brennan estate.

"Anything else you tell me about Ruth?" I asked.

"Not much more than what I've already said. She's been asking around about Maya's previous clients, but she's been careful about how she asks."

"Did she mention Maya in particular?"

"No, and I didn't ask."

I thought about the implications. If Ruth was conducting a professional investigation into Maya's activities, then we weren't the only ones who suspected that Maya's previous clients had died under suspicious circumstances.

"What about Walter?" I asked.

She shook her head.

"Do we have her contact information?" I asked. "Is there a way to reach her?"

"No. She has almost no digital footprint. She's kept her personal information online to a minimum. I don't even have her address. I'm sure Maya would have that information, though. And we know where she is on Mondays and Thursdays. "

14

FALSE ACCUSATIONS

I WAS BACK IN MY CAR, STILL PROCESSING HEATHER'S revelations about Ruth Webb, when my phone rang. It was Kate.

"Harry, we've got a situation. Walter Brennan's condition has deteriorated, and he's making very specific accusations against Maya Santos. You need to get to Memorial, like now."

"Accusations?" I said, frowning.

"He's claiming Maya tried to kill him. Apparently, there was a violent confrontation witnessed by hospital staff. The attending physician wants us to arrest Maya for attempted murder."

I felt that familiar surge of adrenaline. After everything Heather had told me about Ruth's investigation, Walter's accusations could be the break we needed or part of an elaborate setup to frame Maya while protecting the real killers.

"Is Maya still at the hospital?"

"Yes, she's here, demanding to see Walter. Hospital

security has her in the family waiting area, but she's getting agitated. Harry, something about this feels wrong."

"Wrong? how?" I asked.

"Maya's behavior doesn't match someone who just tried to commit murder. She seems genuinely confused and frightened."

I picked up my pace toward the hospital. "What exactly did Walter claim happened?"

"According to Walter, Maya came to his room around two PM claiming she needed to give him medication. When he refused, saying he didn't trust her, she became violent and tried to force some pills down his throat."

"Was anyone else present?"

"That's the problem," Kate replied. "The incident supposedly happened when the charge nurse was dealing with an emergency. By the time staff responded to Walter's call button, Maya was gone and Walter was in severe distress; rapid heartbeat, difficulty breathing, extreme agitation. They had to sedate him. He's conscious now, but terrified. He keeps saying Maya is trying to finish what she started."

I parked the car and ran into the hospital and up to the fourth floor where I found Kate, flanked by two uniformed officers, waiting for me.

"Where's Maya now?" I asked.

"Still in the waiting area. But Harry, she's telling a completely different story. Maya claims she never went to Walter's room today. Says she's been in the waiting area since visiting hours started at noon."

"Can we verify that?" I asked.

"That's the problem. The waiting area was busy. No one specifically remembers seeing Maya continuously, but no one saw her leave either. Ah, he's the Doctor."

"Docter Peterson," Kate said as she approached, "this is Harry Starke, the private investigator I mentioned."

Peterson looked tired but troubled. "Mister Starke, I've been treating Walter Brennan since his admission, and his condition has been puzzling from the beginning."

I frowned. "How so?"

"His symptoms don't match any single medical condition. Initially, we were looking at cardiac issues and medication interactions. But his episodes seem triggered by psychological stress rather than physical illness."

"What about the medication his caregiver allegedly tried to force him to take?" I asked.

"That's where the story becomes problematic. Maya Santos isn't allowed to administer medications here. She'd have no legitimate reason to bring pills to Walter's room."

Kate looked up from her notes. "What's your assessment of Walter's mental state?"

"Complex," Peterson replied. "Walter shows signs of paranoid ideation, but his thinking is clear when he discusses specific events. His fears about being poisoned are detailed and consistent."

"And his accusations against Maya?" she asked.

"They're specific and emotionally compelling," she

replied, "but they don't align with hospital protocols or Maya's known activities today."

I studied Peterson's expression. Her assessment seemed professionally objective, focused on the medical facts rather than personal opinions.

"Could someone have given Walter the impression that Maya was trying to poison him?" I asked.

Peterson wrinkled her brow. "What do you mean?"

"Could someone else have entered his room claiming to be Maya?" I asked. "Could Walter's condition make him mistake one person for another?"

Peterson considered carefully. "Walter's vision is good for his age, and his cognitive function is generally intact. It would be... unusual for him to mistake a stranger for someone he knows well. But extreme stress can cause perceptual distortions."

Kate gestured toward the waiting area. "Harry, I think you and I should talk to Maya before we make any arrest decisions."

We found Maya Santos in a corner chair, looking smaller and more vulnerable than I'd ever seen her. She'd been crying, her professional composure replaced by genuine fear and confusion.

"Ms. Santos," I said, taking a seat across from her and leaning forward, "can you tell me what happened today?"

Maya looked up with red-rimmed eyes. "I came to visit Mr. Brennan during regular visiting hours. I signed in, came to the waiting area, and asked when I could see him."

"Did you go to his room?" Kate asked.

"I never got the chance. The nurses said he was having a difficult day and visitors were restricted. I've been sitting here waiting since noon."

"Maya," I said, gently. "Walter claims you came to his room and tried to force him to take medication."

Maya's expression shifted to bewilderment. "That's impossible. I don't have any medications, and I'm not allowed to give Mr. Brennan anything here. The nurses control his care."

"So you never went to his room today?" I said, leaning back in my chair.

"I just told you that," she said. "I never left this waiting area except to use the restroom and get coffee. You can check with the nurses. I asked them several times when I'd be allowed to visit."

I studied Maya's body language. Either she was an exceptional liar, or she was telling the truth. Her confusion seemed genuine.

"Maya, is there anyone who can verify what you're telling us?"

She thought for a moment, then said, "I talked to some of the other visitors, the volunteers at the information desk, the nurses when I asked about visiting. I wasn't trying to hide. I was just waiting like any other visitor."

"Harry," Kate said, "I checked with the floor nurses. They confirm Maya asked about visiting Walter several times throughout the afternoon. But they can't verify she never left the waiting area."

"What about other security cameras?" I asked. "We need to tie this down, if we can."

"Hospital security is reviewing the footage now, but it's going to take time. The system covers dozens of hallways and stairwells. It could take a couple hours."

If Maya was telling the truth, the cameras would show her in the waiting area. If Walter's accusations were accurate, they'd show Maya entering and leaving his room.

"Kate, what's your instinct?"

"Something doesn't add up. Walter's accusations are specific, but Maya's story is consistent with staff observations. Either Walter's having some kind of psychological episode, or someone else was in his room claiming to be Maya."

"Or someone's manipulating the situation to make Maya look guilty."

Kate nodded. "If Maya is part of a—"

My phone buzzed with a text from an unknown number: *Maya Santos is innocent. The real killer is still free and planning to eliminate Walter tonight. Meet me in the hospital parking garage, level B2, northwest corner. Now. Come alone. - Ruth Webb*

I showed the message to Kate. "Geez," she muttered. "Harry, this could be a trap. If Ruth is really Helen Foster's niece, she might be working with Maya's network."

"Or she might have information that could save Walter's life," I replied, thoughtfully.

"Either way, you're not going alone. Samson and I are coming."

"The message said come alone," I said.

"That message came from someone who's been

hiding from us for days. That doesn't mean we should trust her enough to walk into a potentially dangerous situation without backup."

Kate was right to be cautious, but Ruth's message suggested Walter was in immediate danger and Maya's arrest might be part of someone else's plan.

"Kate, what if you and Samson position yourselves where you can observe and t intervene if necessary?"

"That might work. Level B2 has limited exits, so we could control access while allowing you to meet with Ruth."

As we took the elevator to the parking garage, I could feel the tension building, and so, apparently, could Samson. His ears were pricke, and he seemed to be on full alert. And I have to tell you that that made me feel a little more secure. And, if Ruth was telling the truth, we were about to meet the one person who might save Walter's life. If she was lying, I could well be walking into a trap.

The northwest corner of level B2 was dimly lit and isolated. Kate and Samson positioned themselves behind a concrete pillar where they could observe without being seen, we hoped.

Ruth Webb emerged from behind a parked van, looking nervous but determined. She was younger than I'd expected, in her early thirties, I thought, with a watchful alertness that suggested she'd been living with fear.

"Mister Starke, thank you for coming. Walter Brennan is going to die tonight unless we stop the real killer."

I stared at her for a moment. She seemed sincere, if a little tense. "And who is the real killer?" I asked, finally.

"Someone who's been manipulating this entire investigation from the beginning. Maya Santos is just a pawn. Walter's accusations against her are part of the plan to eliminate him while she takes the blame."

Ruth handed me a large manila envelope. "This is everything Helen, my aunt, and I discovered before she was killed. The actual killer has been using Maya as a scapegoat while positioning themselves to inherit Walter's fortune."

"Ruth, why should I believe you? You've been hiding for days, if not weeks, and now you show up with evidence that supposedly clears Maya?"

"Because Maya Santos is going to be found dead in her apartment tonight, apparently having committed suicide out of guilt. And Walter is going to die of apparent heart failure brought on by stress from the attack."

If she was right, Maya and Walter were both going to be eliminated tonight as part of someone's plan to claim eighty million dollars.

"Who's behind this, Ruth?" I asked.

"I... I don't exactly know. Someone with access to Walter's medical care, someone who can manipulate his medications and condition, someone who can make Maya appear guilty while eliminating all the other witnesses."

"Ruth, you've got to be more specific. Who do you think is planning to kill Walter and Maya tonight?"

She hesitated for a moment, shook her head, then said, "If you want to save Walter's life, you need to get him out of that hospital right now."

"Based on what evidence?" I asked.

Ruth opened the envelope and showed me several documents and said, "These are medical records showing Walter's medications have been systematically altered. Financial records showing payments to Maya that correspond to his declining health. Surveillance photos showing meetings between people who have access to untraceable drugs."

The photos weren't much use; the people in them were unrecognizable, but the rest of the evidence looked compelling. Even so, I couldn't verify its authenticity in a parking garage. She could be telling the truth, or she could be part of an elaborate deception to protect Maya by implicating someone else.

"Ruth, I need you to come with me and present this evidence to Captain Gazzara. We can protect you."

She shook her head. "No, I can't trust anyone connected to the official investigation. Helen thought she could trust the police, and she died for it."

"Then what do you want me to do?" I asked, perplexed.

"Get Walter out of the hospital. Take him somewhere safe where they can't reach him. Once Walter is protected, I'll provide evidence that will expose the entire operation."

She seemed genuine, but her refusal to identify the killer was troubling. Either she was genuinely terrified and trying to save Walter's life, or she was part of a sophisticated plan to manipulate our investigation.

"Ruth, if you really have evidence that someone is planning to kill Walter tonight, you need to tell me who it is right now."

"I've told you everything I can safely tell you here."

Ruth began walking back toward her van, then turned back. "Mister Starke, Maya Santos will be dead sometime within the next few hours. When that happens, ask yourself who benefits from her death and Walter's deteriorating condition. The answer will tell you who the killer is."

She drove away, leaving me with an envelope full of potentially crucial evidence and a warning that two people were going to die tonight unless I acted on information from a source I couldn't verify.

As I walked back toward the elevators, Kate and Samson came forward to join me.

"Harry, what did she tell you?" Kate asked.

"That Maya and Walter are both going to be killed tonight, and that someone with medical access has been manipulating this entire situation."

"Did she identify the killer?"

"No. She didn't, but she insists we get Walter out of the hospital before midnight."

"Can I see?" Kate asked, holding out her hand.

I handed her the envelope. She took it and looked briefly at the contents, then looked at me and said, "This could be legitimate evidence, or it could be disin-formation. I'm not sure what to do with it. One thing's for certain, we can't just up and haul Walter out of here. There would be hell to pay if we did."

"There' could be hell to pay if we don't," I muttered.

Kate looked at me, nodded, then said, "Either way, we need to take Ruth's warning seriously," I said. "If she's right about the timeline, we have less than eight hours to prevent two murders."

"And if she's wrong?" I asked.

"Then all we'll have done is wasted time chasing false leads," I replied. "But if she's right…" I trailed off. I didn't need to say more. "

As we rode the elevator back to the main floor, I thought about the impossible situation Ruth had created. Her information might be the key to saving Walter's life, but acting on it required trusting someone who'd refused to cooperate and whose motives remained unclear.

The stakes couldn't have been higher, and time was running out. We had to make the right decision about whether Ruth Webb was Walter Brennan's salvation or the final piece in an elaborate conspiracy designed to commit the perfect murder.

15

THE SETUP UNRAVELS

BACK IN THE HOSPITAL, KATE AND I FOUND TIM IN THE security office. Two laptops and a tablet added to the bank of security monitors had transformed the small space into a something of a command center.

"Tim, I need you to examine these documents immediately," I said, handing him Ruth's envelope. "They could be elaborate forgeries."

Tim looked up from the security monitor he'd been studying. "Harry, I've got good news and bad news about today's hospital incident. Good news is the security cameras clearly show Maya Santos never left the family waiting area during the time Walter claims she attacked him."

"I was thinking that might be the case," I said. "Go on."

"The bad news is someone did enter Walter's room during that time, and whoever it was knew how to avoid most of the security cameras."

Kate leaned over Tim's shoulder. "Show me," she said.

Tim pulled up several video feeds. "At 2:17 PM, someone in scrubs and a surgical mask enters the stairwell on the east side of Walter's floor. They never appear on main corridor cameras, so they must have known the layout well enough to avoid detection."

"Could you identify who it was?" Kate asked.

"Not from the footage," Tim replied. "Whoever it was was careful to keep their face turned away, they also wore a surgical cap that covered their hair, and moved like they belonged there. Confident, professional."

Tim opened the envelope containing Ruth's 'evidence,' did that thing with his glassed, stared at them for a moment, then said, "Maybe these documents can provide us with a clue," he muttered as he spread the papers out across the desk.

I leaned over to get a better look. There were copies of medical records, prescription logs, lab results, and financial documents.

"What are you seeing, Tim?" Kate asked.

"The papers look good to me," he replied, "though I'd need to make a more thorough examination to be sure. It looks like someone has been altering Walter's medications incrementally over the past three months. Not enough to cause immediate death, but enough to create symptoms of declining health and mental confusion."

Tim pointed to a series of prescription modifications. "Look at this pattern. Walter's digitalis dosage has been increased four times since Maya started caring for him, but each increase was small enough to appear like routine adjustment."

"And digitalis can be lethal in high doses." Kate said.

"Right," Tim said, turning his head to look up at her. "And it causes exactly the symptoms Walter's been experiencing, weakness, confusion, cardiac irregularities. But this is what's really interesting. These blood tests show Walter's digitalis levels have been consistently higher than what his prescribed dosage should produce. It looks like someone's been boosting his dosage."

"Maya?" I asked.

"Ehhh, I dunno," he said, squinting at the paperwork. "Maybe that's what someone wants us to think. Maybe it was her. But look at this. The timing of these payments doesn't correspond to Walter's medication changes. Maya's been getting paid for something, but what? "

Kate studied the timeline. "Hmm, so Maya's been getting paid, but for what?"

"Good question," Tim said. "These payments could be for information, for access, for cooperation, for... anything, even the actual poisoning. There's no way of telling. His prescriptions—medications—have been altered or supplemented by someone with access to his medical records. That could be Maya or... I dunno."

"Tim, who would have the access and knowledge to manipulate Walter's medications this way?" Kate asked.

"Could be several people. A physician with access to his records, a pharmacist handling his prescriptions, someone at the hospital with access to his chart, even someone with connections to Maya's previous employers."

"So we're still looking at multiple possibilities," Kate muttered.

"Right," Tim replied. This evidence—if you can call it that—is ambiguous, to say the least. It doesn't point to any specific individual."

Kate's phone rang. She answered it, "Gazzara!"

"Captain Gazzara? This is Doctor Peterson at Memorial Hospital. We have an emergency here and, considering the situation, I thought you should know it."

"Hold on, Doctor," Kate said and put the call on speaker. "What kind of emergency?"

"Walter Brennan has suffered what appears to be a severe cardiac event. His condition deteriorated rapidly about twenty minutes ago, and he's currently in critical condition in the cardiac care unit."

"Geez," she replied. "That's not good. Is he going to survive?"

"It's too early to tell. His vital signs are unstable. But Captain, there's something else. We found a syringe under the bed in his room. It isn't one of ours and a preliminary analysis confirmed it contained concentrated digitalis solution. It appears someone tried to kill him and dropped the syringe in the process."

"Dr. Peterson," I said, leaning nearer to the phone. "This is Harry Starke. Do you know where Maya Santos is now?"

"No, I haven't seen her," she replied.

"Dr. Peterson, we need to secure Walter's room immediately," Kate said. No one is to have access until I get there.

"Already done," she replied. "Hospital security has posted guards, and we've restricted access to Walter's care team."

The moment Kate hung up, we were moving; no discussion needed. When someone tries to kill your primary witness, you get to them fast.

"Tim, you stay here and continue analyzing Ruth's so-called evidence," I said as we headed for the door. "Monitor all communications and let us know if anything changes."

"Got it," he replied. "I'll call if I find anything urgent."

Kate and I took the elevator up to Walter's floor, Samson at Kate's heels. The hallway was buzzing with activity: nurses, security guards, and what looked like a hospital administrator discussing protocols in hushed tones.

Dr. Peterson met us outside Walter's room. She looked tired but relieved. "He's stable now. We got the digitalis out of his system in time, but it was close."

"Can we see him?" Kate asked.

"Briefly. He's conscious but weak."

Walter looked pale against the white hospital sheets, but his eyes were clear and focused when we entered. He tried to sit up when he saw us.

"Easy, Mr. Brennan," I said. "How are you feeling?"

"Like someone tried to poison me," he replied, his voice hoarse. "Which they did, didn't they?"

Kate nodded. "Do you remember anything? Anyone coming into your room who shouldn't have been here?"

Walter closed his eyes for a moment, then said, "There was a nurse I'd not seen before. About an hour before I started feeling sick. Said she needed to check my IV medications."

So it was a woman, I thought. "Can you describe her?" I asked.

He squinted up at me and I got the impression that if he could have shrugged, he would have. "Middle-aged," he said, "blonde, I think, wearing scrubs and a mask like everyone else. But she seemed nervous, kept looking toward the door like she was worried about being interrupted."

"And you're sure you haven't seen her before?" I asked.

He frowned. "No, I don't think so. It's possible. She was wearing a mask and, and one of those blue head covers. All I could see was her eyes."

"If she was wearing a head cover, how d'you know she was blonde?" Kate asked.

He tilted his head as he looked up at her. "The was a strand of hair hanging out over her left ear."

Dr. Peterson frowned. "I don't know of any middle-aged blonde nurses on the evening shift. They're all quite young."

I turned to Kate. "I'll call Tim and have him ask security to check the footage. We need to see who entered the room during the last two hours."

My phone buzzed with a text from Ruth. *Where the hell is she?* I wondered as I opened it.

Walter's attack wasn't random, it read. *What did I tell you? You didn't believe me, did you? Maya Santos is supposed to die tonight too. Someone is cleaning up loose ends.*

I showed the message to Kate.

"Yeah, she already told you," Kate said, sounding totally frustrated.

Before I could answer, an alarm started blaring. A nurse rushed past our doorway, followed by what looked like a crash team.

"That's coming from the ICU," Dr. Peterson said, his face pale. "It's at the end of the hall next to the service elevators." She took out her phone and punched in a number. "This is Doctor Peterson. What's happening?"

She listened for a minute, then ended the call, looked at me and said, "It's Maya Santo. She tried to commit suicide."

We ran down the hallway, leaving Samson with the security guard outside Walter's room. The ICU was chaos - medical staff working frantically around Maya's bed while monitors showed dangerously erratic vital signs.

"What's Maya's condition?" Kate asked the charge nurse while at the same time showing her her badge.

"Critical," the nurse replied. "She was found unconscious in her car in the hospital parking lot about ten minutes ago. A paramedic spotted her during shift change and called for help."

"Suicide attempt?" Kate asked.

"That's what it looks like," the nurse replied. "She took a massive dose of benzodiazepine. Some of it was still in her mouth. There was also a suicide note on the passenger seat confessing to poisoning Walter and murdering Helen Foster and James Morrison. The hospital administrator has it."

I took a deep breath and shook my head. This was exactly what Ruth had warned us about, but was Maya being set up to take the fall?

"Will she survive?" I asked.

The nurse looked grim. "It's too early to tell. The next twelve hours will be critical. She's unconscious and will be for at least that long, maybe longer, if she pulls through."

Kate was already on the phone to Mike Willis, the department's CSI supervisor. "...I want that suicide note processed for fingerprints and handwriting analysis. And I want the car towed and processed ASAP. Get copies of the security footage from the parking lot..."

It was at that point my phone rang - Ruth again, her voice tight with fear.

"Mr. Starke, I saw what happened to Maya. You need to know it wasn't suicide... She is dead, isn't she?"

"Not quite," I replied. "It's touch and go, but it looks like she might survive. Where are you, Ruth?"

"Maya was supposed to die and leave behind evidence that made her look guilty," she said, ignoring my question. "But if she survives, and Walter survives... With both of them surviving, whoever's behind this is going to have to try something more direct."

"Ruth, you need to come in and tell us what you know," I said. "Where are you?"

"I can't come in," she replied, ignoring my question for the second time. Not yet. But I'm watching the hospital, and there are people here who shouldn't be."

"People?" I frowned. "What people?"

"The kind who have a lot to lose if this investigation continues. Be careful, Mr. Starke. This is bigger than just Maya taking advantage of an old man."

The line went dead. Kate was watching me, having caught the tail end of the conversation.

"Ruth thinks there are people inside the hospital who are connected to this mess," I told her. "I asked her where she was but she wouldn't tell me, other than she watching the place. Geez!"

"Then we better find them, and quick," Kate said.

As we walked back toward Walter's room to coordinate security, I suddenly realized that someone had just made a critical mistake. By trying to eliminate both Walter, and especially Maya, and on the same night, they'd revealed that this wasn't about a single caregiver acting alone; it was a conspiracy, and the perpetrators were now scrambling to cover their tracks.

The question was, of course, whether we could identify them before they could kill again.

16

HIDDEN MOTIVES

THE REVELATION THAT SOMEONE HAD BEEN orchestrating events to frame Maya while eliminating Walter forced us to completely reconsider our approach. With both intended victims surviving their attempted murders, we now had a chance to uncover the real conspiracy behind what had previously looked like simple elder abuse.

Tim had worked through the night, analyzing Ruth's evidence and cross-referencing it with our own financial and medical records and when Kate and I returned to our makeshift command center the next morning, we found him surrounded by printouts, charts, and his two laptops, their screens displaying complex data.

"Harry, Kate, you need to see this," he said, turning around in his chair, his eyes bright.

We sat down, one on either side of him. Samson parked himself next to Kate's chair and lay down, his chin on the floor between his paws, looking thoroughly bored.

"The financial trail behind the payments Maya's been receiving is quite sophisticated," Tim began, pointing to a flowchart that looked like something from a federal investigation. "The money comes through at least three different shell companies, two offshore accounts, and two intermediary firms. Whoever set this up has serious resources."

"What kind of resources?" I asked.

"Well, you need this kind of setup only if you have something to hide," he said. "This kind of sophistication suggests organized criminal activity. The payment structure is designed to be completely untraceable, and it's been operating for over two years."

Tim showed me records of similar payment patterns in Atlanta, Houston, Birmingham, and Memphis, all cities where Maya had previously worked as a caregiver for elderly clients who died under suspicious circumstances.

"Maya Santos has been receiving payments from this network for over two years, but the amounts and timing suggest she's not the primary beneficiary."

"What do you mean, Tim?" Kate asked.

"Maya's been receiving four thousand a month a month on top of what she's paid by her clients, and she's been receiving inheritance money, property transfers, insurance settlements, but she doesn't keep them, at least not as as far as I can tell. The money and assets disappeared from her accounts almost as soon as she received them, and I can't trace them."

Kate leaned forward. "So Maya must be working for someone else, then; as we suspect?"

"That's what the evidence suggests," Tim replied. "Maya's being paid to provide access, information, and cooperation, but someone else has been making the major decisions and reaping the primary benefits."

He pulled up another screen showing property records and estate transfers. "Look at this pattern. In each city where Maya worked, elderly clients changed their wills to benefit her, but then Maya signed over significant portions of her inheritance to various business entities and investment funds."

"So she's been laundering the money?" Kate asked, frowning.

"You could say that?" Tim replied. "Or she's being forced to transfer it to her employers. Maya would inherit fifty thousand here, a hundred thousand there, but then she'd immediately sign contracts transferring most of the money to shell companies."

Kate looked at me. I slowly shook my head. I was thinking that Maya wasn't the serial killer targeting elderly victims we thought she was. She was simply a low-level employee in a sophisticated criminal organization that specialized in systematic elder abuse and inheritance fraud.

"Tim, do you have any idea who's behind this organization?" I asked.

"That's what I've been trying to figure out all night," he replied, obviously frustrated. "The paper trail is incredibly complex, but there are patterns that suggest the operation is based here in Tennessee, possibly with connections to legitimate businesses in medical and legal fields."

"Geez," I muttered, also frustrated.

"Look here," Tim said, flipping through the screens until he found the one he was looking for. "These documents indicate at least one of the shell companies is connected to professional services firms in Nashville, Knoxville, and Chattanooga."

"That's an elder care company," I said, staring at the screen. There were nine different service providers, including an investment broker, two real estate brokers, and... "Tim, that one... Isn't that the one that's been handling Walter's will? Is there anything to indicate these companies are not legitimate entities?"

"No, not that I can see, but that doesn't mean there are not individuals within them that are, I dunno. Involved?"

I sat back in my chair and stared at the two laptop screens. For several minutes, no one spoke, and then Tim said, "But I did find something interesting about Walter's case." He flipped to another screen, then continued, "Walter's situation differs from Maya's previous victims in several important ways."

"How so?" I asked, frowning.

"First, Walter's estate is much larger. We're talking eighty million versus the fifty thousand to quarter-million estates she's been working so far. Second, Walter's will change was more dramatic; usually Maya inherited a portion, but Walter left her everything."

"What else?" I asked, staring at the screen.

"I think there's evidence Walter's case was planned much more carefully and over a longer time period. The systematic medication changes, the gradual isolation from family, the careful documentation of his declining mental state." He shrugged. "Beats me," he finished.

"Tim, if Maya's just... lets say an employee, then who made the decision to target Walter?"

"That's a good question," he replied. "And the short answer is, I don't know, but it had to have been someone with detailed knowledge of his financial situation, his family dynamics, and his medical conditions. I don't think the targeting wasn't random. I think Walter was selected because he met a specific criteria." Tim consulted his notes. "He had substantial assets, minimal family oversight, existing health conditions that could explain declining mental and physical function, and social isolation that would make it difficult for him to seek help."

I sighed heavily. "Walter certainly fits that profile," I said.

My phone rang. I looked at the screen. I recognized the number. It was Ruth's.

"Ms. Webb," I said. "Where are you?" I asked as I put the phone on speaker and nodded to Kate.

"Never mind that," she replied. "I've been watching hospital. Mr. Starke, I've managed to identify two of the people I saw here yesterday .One of them is Thomas McKinnon, an attorney who specializes in estate planning and elder law. He has offices in Atlanta and Nashville, and he's been involved in probate proceedings for several of Maya's previous clients."

I didn't like the sound of that. An attorney with connections to several victims suggested complicity.

"And the other one?" I asked.

"The woman is Patricia Stevens," she replied. "She works for a company called Senior Care Consulting Services. They provide financial and medical management services for elderly clients, and they've also been involved in managing assets for people who died while Maya was taking care of them."

I looked at Kate. She was taking notes.

"Mr. Starke, this isn't just about Maya or Walter," she said. "I think what we have here is an organized operation that has been defrauding and possibly murdering elderly people for years."

I frowned. "How d'you know all this, Ms. Webb? And how many victims—?"

She cut me off. "Helen and I have been working on it for months until she... Until they murdered her. As to how many victims? Probably dozens."

"Ms. Webb," I said, thinking out loud, "what d'you know about McKinnon and Stevens?"

"Helen had extensive documentation, but... As far as I can tell, McKinnon handled the legal aspects—will changes, estate planning, probate proceedings, and so forth. Stevens managed the medical and care coordination—finding caregivers like Maya, arranging medical services, coordinating with healthcare providers. And they're both connected to several shell companies and investment vehicles that receive the inheritance money."

Kate looked up from her notes. "Ms. Webb, if this is such a large operation, there must be other people involved, right?"

"That's what Helen was trying to figure out when she died," Webb replied. "She suspected there were a lot of people in positions of authority who were either actively participating or being paid to look the other way."

I leaned back in my chair and blew air out through my lips. The scope of the conspiracy was becoming clearer, but also more troubling. If Ruth and Helen were correct, we were dealing with a criminal organization that had infiltrated multiple professional fields and had been operating with impunity for years.

"Ruth, why did this organization target Walter specifically?" I asked. "His case seems different from their usual pattern."

"The difference is that Walter was supposed to be their biggest score. Eighty million in one hit is more than they'd typically get from five or six smaller jobs. But Walter's case also represented a test of whether they could handle high-value targets without attracting attention."

"And now that their plan has failed?" Kate murmured.

"Now they're scrambling to minimize their exposure and eliminate anyone who can connect them to the failed operation," she said, "Which is why Maya was supposed to die, as well as Walter, and that was supposed to be the end of it."

"But it's not, is it?" I said. "If Maya survives and testifies…" I trailed off. The implication was clear enough. They couldn't afford that.

"Which is why they're going to try to eliminate her again," Kate said. "Maya knows too much. She knows who's been paying her, and how the operation works. She's the key witness who could bring down everyone involved. We need to increase Maya's security immediately. I'll have uniform send a couple of officers." He stood, walked away a few steps and made the call, then she returned to her seat. Samson lifted his head, blinked at her, then laid it down again.

"What about Walter?" I said.

"Yeah, for him, too," she replied, already at the door.

I remained seated, thinking about the implications. Maya Santos wasn't the villain we'd thought she was. Was she was a victim of an organization that had exploited her and involved her in systematic elder abuse and murder? At that point, there was no knowing. What we did know was that she was the key witness whose testimony could expose a criminal conspiracy that had been operating for years.

"Ruth, I need you to come in," I said. "We can protect you, but we need your testimony and Helen's documentation to build a case."

"I can't do that yet. There are still people involved in this mess who we haven't identified, people in positions of authority who could suppress evidence or eliminate witnesses. Someone killed my aunt Helen, and I don't think it was Maya. So, until we know who they are, it's not safe for me."

"I get it," I replied. "So, how do you want to proceed?"

"I think you need to focus on protecting Maya and Walter," she replied. "And you need to gather evidence against the people we can identify—McKinnon, Stevens, and whoever else is directly involved. Once you have enough evidence to ensure successful prosecutions, I'll come forward with everything Helen and I discovered."

As Ruth ended the call, Kate and I looked at each other, then Kate said, "Harry, if this organization has been operating for as long as we think they have, they've probably developed contingency plans for just this kind of situation."

"Yeah, I know what you mean," I muttered in a tone of voice that made Samson jerk his head up, then stand and walk around Tim and shove that huge, cold, wet nose into my hand.

"Right," Kate said. "The people behind this operation have millions of dollars and multiple reputations at stake."

Tim had been silent for the last several minutes, still analyzing data, but then he looked up and said, "This organization, if that's what it is, isn't simply targeting random elderly people. They seem to be focusing on clients of specific medical practices and legal firms."

I frowned. "You want to explain that, Tim?"

"Well, from what I can tell, most, if not all, the victims have been patients of a select group of physicians and attorneys. The targeting appears to be coordinated through professional networks rather than random opportunity."

"Go on," I said.

"At the very least, someone with access to medical records and financial information has been feeding information to McKinnon and Stevens."

The implications were stunning. If members of the medical and legal communities were actively participating in this conspiracy, then no elderly person with substantial assets was safe from exploitation and potential murder.

"Tim, we need to identify which local professionals are involved, if any. If they know we're closing in, they might try to clean up their act by destroying evidence and eliminating witnesses."

"Starting with Maya and Walter," Kate said

"Yeah, them," I muttered. "And possibly us, too."

"I'm on it," Tim said, hunched over his equipment.

Samson had been resting quietly, got up and wandered over to the window. Kate stopped staring at the security screens and went to join him, staring out over the hospital parking lot.

"Harry," she said suddenly, "there's a van in the parking lot. It was there more than an hour ago. There are people in the front seats. They don't look like hospital staff or visitors. I think they're conducting surveillance."

Tim looked over at her, then quickly accessed the hospital's external security cameras and zoomed in on the suspicious vehicle. "There are at least three people in that van," he said, "and Kate's right, fast reversing the footage. It looks like... They arrived at 07:05 this morning, and they've just been sitting there. "

"McKinnon's people?" I wondered out loud.

"Or Stevens's, or both," Kate replied. "Either way, they could simply be waiting for the go to finish off Maya and Walter. I'm calling in backup!" She took out her phone and made the call.

"They're on the way," she said, after ending the call. "If these people are desperate enough to conduct surveillance in broad daylight, who knows what else they're capable of? And if they're planning to take out Maya and Walter..." she trailed off, looking at me.

"They might go after us," I finished for her.

While Kate coordinated with responding units from the window, and Tim continued to monitor the security feeds, I had a feeling the investigation had reached a critical juncture, and that the next few hours would determine whether we could gather enough evidence to prosecute the conspiracy before its members could eliminate the witnesses and possibly the investigators who threatened their operation. With millions of dollars at stake and multiple lives hanging in the balance, we were engaged in a high-stakes game where the wrong move could result in multiple deaths.

Maya Santos and Walter Brennan had survived one attempt on their lives, but the people behind this conspiracy weren't going to give up easily. They had too much to lose and plenty of resources at their disposal to simply accept defeat. And I had to wonder if our small team of investigators would be able to outmaneuver a well-funded, professionally organized criminal enterprise that had been perfecting its methods for years and had connections throughout the medical and legal communities that were supposed to protect vulnerable elderly people from exactly this kind of exploitation.

17

THE THIRD DEATH

I was at breakfast with Amanda and Jade the next morning when my phone rang. I looked at the screen and saw it was Kate. I accepted the call and said, "What now, Kate?"

"Walter Brennan died an hour ago, Harry," she replied, sounding more than a little frustrated. "You need to get down here."

I felt like I'd been punched in the stomach. After everything we'd done to protect Walter, after him surviving the digitalis injection and systematic poisoning, it was all for nothing; he was gone.

"Oh no," I couldn't help but say. "What the hell happened, Kate?" I looked at Amanda. She was staring at me. So was Jade, with her spoon in her mouth.

"Apparently, it was heart failure," she replied. "The attending physician said Walter's condition had been deteriorating throughout the night, and his heart simply couldn't handle the stress."

"Was anyone with him when he died?" I asked.

"The night shift nurse checked on him at five and found him unresponsive. They attempted resuscitation, but they think he'd probably been dead for a while. They'll do an autopsy, of course."

"Kate, this can't be natural," I said. "Not now, not after everything we've discovered."

"My thoughts exactly," she replied. "But Harry, the preliminary examination suggests Walter died of cardiac arrest consistent with his existing medical condition."

"What about security?" I asked. "Was anyone else on the floor who shouldn't have been there? What about your officers? Did they see anything?"

"That's what we're trying to figure out. Hospital security is reviewing all the footage from last night, but preliminary reports suggest no unauthorized personnel had access to or entered Walter's room."

I thought for a minute, then said, "Okay, I'm on my way. I need a few minutes. I'll be there at…" I looked at my watch. "By eight." And I ended the call.

Amanda was watching me. "Walter?" she asked quietly.

I nodded, "He died," I muttered.

"Oh, Harry," she said as she reached out across the table and squeezed my hand.

I nodded, rose to my feet, slipped into my shoulder rig and blue suit jacket, then kissed them both and headed out the door, my mind in a whirl.

"Be careful out there," she called after me.

The drive to Memorial Hospital gave me time to think about what Walter's death meant. He'd been our primary victim, the person whose testimony could have confirmed the systematic poisoning and abuse. With him gone, our case against the criminal conspiracy became much more dependent on Maya Santos.

The hospital was quieter than usual, but there was an undercurrent of tension among the staff. Kate met me at the main entrance with Samson at her side.

"What do we know so far?" I asked as we walked toward the elevator.

"Walter was stable when the evening shift ended at eleven last night," she replied. The night shift nurse checked on him every two hours per her instructions. At three o'clock he was sleeping peacefully with normal vital signs."

"And at five?" I asked.

"The nurse found him unresponsive. No signs of struggle, no indication that anyone else had been in the room. The monitoring equipment showed his heart rate and blood pressure declining gradually over about thirty minutes before he went into cardiac arrest."

As soon as we reached Walter's floor, we were approached by a Dr. Roberts, the attending physician. He had that tired look of someone who'd been dealing with death and uncertainty throughout a long night.

"Mister Starke and Captain Gazzara, I presume," he said, holding out his hand to Kate. "I'm sorry we couldn't save him. Walter's condition has been precarious since the digitalis poisoning, and his heart was severely compromised."

"Have you any idea what might have caused his

sudden deterioration between three and five this morning, Doctor?" I asked. "Could it have been induced?"

"Was he murdered, you mean?" he asked.

I nodded.

"I don't think so," he replied. "Based on his condition and medical history, cardiac arrest was always a significant risk. The poisoning had damaged his cardiovascular system, and the stress of recent events had pushed his body beyond its ability to recover. Having said that..." he hesitated for a moment, then continued, "It's possible that any additional stress on his system—physical, emotional, or pharmacological—could have triggered the cardiac event that killed him."

I leaned forward slightly. "And?"

"Another dose of medication," he said quietly, "even something as simple as a sedative or pain reliever, could have been enough to push Walter's compromised system into failure. But without an autopsy, we can't determine if anything like that occurred."

Kate looked up from her notebook and said, "Doctor, what about the security protocols that were in place? Could someone have accessed Walter's room without being detected?"

"The official protocols were followed, and there was an officer present outside his door," he replied. "Walter's room was monitored, and only authorized medical personnel had access. But hospitals are complex environments, and someone with knowledge of our procedures could easily find ways to circumvent security measures… by posing as a doctor or nurse, for instance."

That was troubling, but not unexpected. If the criminal conspiracy included medical professionals, they would understand exactly how to navigate hospital security.

"In the circumstances, Doctor Roberts," Kate said, "I have to treat Mister Brennan's death as suspicious. That being so, we're going to need a complete autopsy to determine Walter's exact cause of death."

"I understand," he replied. "The hospital pathologist has already been notified, and Walter's body will be transferred for comprehensive examination."

As Roberts returned to his duties, Kate and I walked to Walter's room, where hospital security was conducting their investigation. The room looked exactly as it should: medical equipment properly positioned, no signs of disturbance, nothing to suggest anything unusual had occurred.

"Harry, if someone killed Walter, we have a real problem."

"That, Kate, is an understatement," I replied thoughtfully. "If that's what happened, it suggests someone with medical expertise and knowledge was able to get to him and induce cardiac arrest—"

It was at that point in the conversation my phone rang. It was Tim.

"Tim, what the hell?" I snapped. "I told you to go home and get some sleep and not to come in until noon."

"Yeah, well, things happen, don't they?" he replied,

caustically. "I got a text from one of hospital security people about Walter's death at five-thirty this morning. Nice lady. I was talking to her all day yesterday. We got along great and I—"

"Tim, for Pete's sake," I said, interrupting him.

"Oh, yeah, sorry," he replied. "Okay, so I asked her to let me know if anything happened and she did, so I came right here. Harry, I've got some troubling news. The surveillance van that was watching the hospital yesterday evening left around midnight, but it was replaced by seral different surveillance teams throughout the night."

"How many teams?" I asked.

"At least three different vehicles and personnel. I dunno, Harry. They looked like pros to me."

"Any idea who they were?" I asked.

"No," he replied. "But based on the license plates and vehicle registrations, the vans are all owned by one of the shell companies that have been funding Maya's payments."

Kate was listening. "Tim, did any of these surveillance teams show unusual activity around the time Walter died?" she asked.

"That's what's interesting. Around four AM, about an hour before Walter was found dead, there was a significant increase in radio communications among the surveillance teams. Like they were coordinating a response to some kind of development. The communications pattern suggests they were either monitoring the hospital frequencies or they had someone inside providing real-time information."

"Tim, what about Maya? Is she still alive?" I asked. *Damn it, I should have asked the Doctor.*

"I'm told that Maya's condition has been stable throughout the night. She's unconscious but responding to treatment for the drug overdose. The doctors think she'll survive, but it's going to be several days before she's able to communicate."

I looked at Kate and said, "Maya's security?"

"There's a uniformed officer on duty at all times," she replied, "and I've alerted the hospital administration to the increased threat. I was told they'd alerted the staff and were taking no chances with their other critical patient."

As Tim ended the call, Kate and I looked at each other.

I shook my head and and said, "We failed him, Kate. We failed to protect him."

"No, Harry," she replied. "We did all we could, but Walter's death changes things. Without his testimony, our evidence becomes much more circumstantial."

"But it also means they, whoever they are, succeeded in eliminating their primary threat."

"Which leaves Maya as the only surviving witness," she said, quietly.

"And Maya is still unconscious," I said, "and she may not remember details when and if she recovers."

Kate walked out into the corridor. Samson ambled out after her, his tongue hanging out the right side of his mouth. She stood for a moment, staring back along the corridor. Samson sat down, looking up at her. Absentmindedly, she reached down and scratched behind his ears, then she seemed to snap out of some sort of reverie and turned to me and said, "Harry, if these people are as ruthless as we think they are, they aren't going to stop at killing Walter, they'll go after Maya, too. "

"You really think they'll go after her with all this enhanced security?" I asked.

"Not only do I think that," she replied. "I think they'll try to eliminate anyone who poses a threat: Maya, Ruth Webb, and maybe even us."

That thought had also occurred to me. These people had tens of millions of dollars at stake, and they'd demonstrated their willingness to commit murder many times over.

"Kate, we need to review everything we know, Kate," I said thoughtfully. "What we have is all circumstantial at best, and iffy at worst. I don't like it one bit. In fact, I have a deep-seated feeling that this case is about to go sideways in a hurry. Without Walter's testimony…" I trailed off, shaking my head.

"What about Ruth's evidence?" she asked.

"Ruth's evidence could be crucial, but we don't have it, and it's not going to be admissible in court until she comes forward officially. And the silly woman is afraid to come forward because she believes there are people in positions of authority who are involved, including your department. She's scared, Kate, and I don't blame her."

We walked back toward the hospital's administrative area, where Tim was still at work. By then it was almost ten o'clock, and the hospital was slowly returning to normal activity, even though there were police officers everywhere. That wasn't a good thing for the hospital, of course, but I have to admit it made me feel a little better, and safer. The hospital was a weapons free area, so I'd left my CZ shadow in the car, and I felt naked and vulnerable without it. Fortunately, though, Samson was at Kate's side and, to my certain knowledge, he'd saved her life a couple of times.

Good lad, I thought, looking down at him. He looked up at me. It was as if he could read my mind and, dammit; he winked at me.

"Tim," I said as we entered the office, "we need to identify everyone involved in this conspiracy as quickly as possible. With Walter dead, we can't ignore the fact that they're going to go after threats, witnesses."

"I've been working on that," Tim replied, gesturing to his laptops and documents. "The good news is that I've identified several more people who appear to be connected to the network funding this operation."

"You have?" I asked. "Who?"

"Besides Thomas McKinnon and Patricia Stevens, there are at least four other professionals who have been involved in handling money, providing services, or facilitating the targeting of victims. Here, take a look."

He showed me a hand-drawn flow chart that showed connections between various individuals and organizations. "Dr. Richard Morrison, a geriatrician in Nashville who's been treating several of victims before their deaths. Sandra McNulty, an estate planning attorney in Birmingham who'd worked with McKinnon on probate proceedings. Michael Torres, a financial advisor in Atlanta who's been managing investments for the shell companies."

"And the fourth person?" I asked.

"That's where it gets interesting," he said, actually grinning. "Someone local who's been coordinating medical services and prescription management for several victims…" He paused, looked up at me, saw the look on my face, then quickly said, "including Walter Brennan."

I felt a surge of mixed emotions, including frustration with Tim and a heightened level of apprehension. "Who, is, it, Tim?"

"Um, yeah, well, I'm not quite sure," he said. "The payments and communication patterns suggest it's someone with broad access to medical records and prescription systems, someone who could alter medications and coordinate care between multiple healthcare providers."

"It's a doctor, then?" I asked, after taking a deep breath.

"Probably," he replied, "but I haven't been able to identify the specific individual yet. The electronic trail is quite sophisticated and appears to have been specifically designed to hide the identity of this particular person."

Kate looked up from the reports she'd been reviewing. "Tim, if this person is local and has been coordinating Walter's care, then it might be someone we've already encountered during the investigation."

"That's what I'm afraid of," he replied. "If it's someone we've already been working with—someone here in the hospital—they've almost certainly been monitoring our investigation."

That was a possibility I didn't even want to contemplate, and t started my mind churning, searching for possibilities. The first that came to mind was Dr. Peterson, then there was the so-called middle-aged blonde nurse that had visited Walter Brennan's room just before he died. *Who the hell was that?* I wondered.

"Tim, I want you to focus on identifying this person," I said. "By now they know we're closing in, and if so—"

I was interrupted by my phone buzzing with a text from Ruth. *By now, you'll know what I told you is correct and that Walter's death was not natural. You have to protect Maya. I still haven't been able to identify the person we're looking for, but if I were you, I'd check the hospital's medical staff. The killer has to be hiding in plain sight. - Ruth*

I showed the message to Kate and Tim.

"That makes sense," Kate said.

"Someone who would have had access to Walter throughout his stay," I said, "someone who could have caused his death without triggering security protocols. That sounds like Dr. Peterson to me... or one of the nurses."

Kate nodded. "The blonde woman."

I turned to Tim, but he was already pulling up hospital personnel records and cross-referencing them with the financial and communication patterns he'd been tracking. "If Ruth is right," he said, "if there's someone on the medical staff who's been coordinating with McKinnon and Stevens, they would have had perfect access to Walter and perfect cover for any actions they took. And maybe their financials will offer a clue as to who it might be."

Kate stood up. "Harry," she said. "I'm worried about Maya. If Walter was murdered by someone on the hospital staff, then Maya's in danger."

"But we also need to be careful about who we trust with this information," I said. "If Ruth is right, and the killer is someone on the medical staff, we can't be sure who's working with us and who's working against us, so we need to tread carefully."

18

THE LOCAL CONNECTION

THE NEXT MORNING BROUGHT A BREAKTHROUGH THAT I hadn't expected. Tim had been working late into the night again, cross-referencing digging into the financial records using the hospital's staff database, and what he'd found was troubling enough to warrant immediate action.

"Harry, Kate," he said as we gathered in the security office, "I think I've identified the person we're looking for."

Kate looked up from reviewing the previous day's security footage. "Who is it?" she asked.

"Dr. Amanda Richardson, internal medicine," Tim replied, pulling up her personnel file on his laptop. "She's been receiving payments through the same shell company network, but here's the strange part: the payments don't correspond to any obvious services."

I studied the photograph on the screen. Dr. Richardson was a woman in her early forties with shoulder-length brown hair and the kind of professional appearance that inspired confidence in patients and colleagues alike. Nothing about her suggested someone capable of systematic murder.

"How much and for how long?" I asked.

"Three thousand a month for eighteen months," Tim replied. "But unlike Maya's payments, there's no clear pattern connecting Richardson's payments to specific patient deaths or care activities."

Kate leaned forward to examine the financial records Tim had compiled. "What kind of medical involvement has she had with suspicious death cases?"

"That's what's odd," Tim said. "She's provided routine consultations on maybe half a dozen elderly patients over the past two years, but nothing that would justify these payments. The consultations were standard medical practice, nothing unusual or suspicious."

"So either she's very good at hiding her involvement, or something else is going on," I said.

Tim nodded. "The payment pattern suggests she's important to the conspiracy, but I can't figure out why."

Kate sat back in her chair, her arms folded across her chest, obviously thinking, staring at the laptop's screen, focused on the discrepancy between the payments and Dr. Richardson's apparent minimal involvement in... something. "Where is she now?" she asked.

"According to the hospital schedule," Tim replied, "she's making her rounds in the cardiac care unit. She's scheduled to be there until eleven."

Kate stood up, startling Samson with the sudden

move. "Let's go talk to her," Kate said. "Maybe she can explain the payments."

"And maybe she's better at covering her tracks than we think," I added as Kate headed for the door with Samson on her heels.

"Come on, Tim," I said. "Bring your laptop."

We made our way to the cardiac care unit, where Dr. Richardson was reviewing charts at the nurses' station. She looked up as we approached, her expression shifting from professional courtesy to mild curiosity as she recognized us from our previous hospital visits.

"Doctor Richardson?" Kate said, showing her badge. "We'd like to speak with you for a moment. Is there somewhere quiet we can go?"

Richardson frowned. "What's this about?"

"It's… about some financial records that have come to our attention," Kate said.

"Financial records?" she replied, looking genuinely puzzled. "I'm not sure why you would want to talk with me."

"We're investigating the death of Walter Brennan," I said, watching her reaction carefully. "Your name has appeared in some financial documents connected to the case."

Richardson's expression shifted to one of concern, and it seemed to me like the natural reaction of someone hearing disturbing news rather than the controlled response of someone trying to hide guilt. "I'm sorry," she said, "but I have no idea what you're talking about. What kind of financial documents?"

"The records show you've been receiving monthly payments of three thousand dollars from an organization called Pinnacle Medical Research," Kate said. "Can you explain those payments?"

"I've never heard of Pinnacle Medical Research," she replied. She sounded both indignant and confused. "I certainly haven't been receiving any payments from them or anyone else outside my hospital salary."

Kate turned her head, looked at Tim, and nodded. He stepped forward with his laptop, showing her the financial records he'd compiled. "Doctor, these bank records show deposits to an account in your name."

She leaned forward to examine the screen, her expression growing more troubled as she studied the information. "This is impossible," she snapped. "I've never opened an account with this bank, and I've certainly never received these payments."

"The account shows your social security number and address," Kate said calmly.

"Then someone has been using my identity fraudulently," Richardson replied, her voice taking on the firm tone of someone who was absolutely certain of their facts. "I have no knowledge of this account or these payments."

I studied her reaction carefully. Either Richardson was an exceptional actress, or she was genuinely shocked by the revelation that payments had been made in her name without her knowledge.

"Have you had any involvement with Maya Santos in connection with elderly patients?" I asked.

"Isn't she Walter Brennan's caregiver?" she replied.

"Yes, I've seen her around the hospital during Mr. Brennan's care, and I've spoken with her at times, but I don't really know her."

"What about your consultation on Mr. Brennan's case?" Kate asked.

"Standard internal medicine consultation. His regular physician, Dr. Walker, wanted a second opinion on his cardiac symptoms and medication interactions. There's nothing unusual about that."

Richardson's answers were consistent and delivered with the confidence of someone telling the truth, but the financial evidence was equally compelling. Someone was lying, and I wasn't sure who.

"Doctor Richardson," I said, "we'd like you to come with us to review this evidence more thoroughly. There are some serious discrepancies that need to be resolved."

"Of course," she replied. "I want to get to the bottom of this as much as you do. If someone has been using my identity, I need to know about it."

We escorted Dr. Richardson to a private conference room near the hospital's administrative offices, where Tim set up his laptop and brought up financial evidence in more detail.

"Doctor," Kate said as we settled around the conference table, "we're going to show you the complete financial records and see if you can help us understand what's been happening."

"I appreciate that," she replied. "But I want to emphasize that I have no knowledge of any payments or accounts in my name that I didn't authorize."

Tim opened the banking records, showing the systematic monthly deposits that had been made to the account bearing Richardson's name and personal information. "These deposits began eighteen months ago and have continued every month since then," he said, turning the laptop so she could see the screen.

Richardson studied the records carefully, her expression growing more concerned as she reviewed the dates and amounts. "This is identity theft," she said, hollowly. "Someone has been using my personal information to create this account and make these deposits. Why would they do that?"

"It's certainly possible that this is a case of identity theft, Doctor," I said. "But we need to understand why someone would target you specifically. Why would someone do that? What would make you a target for this kind of..." I shook my head, then finished lamely, "fraud?"

"I have no idea," she replied. "I'm not particularly wealthy, and I don't have access to anything that would make me an obvious target. Why would someone open a bank account in my name and then make regular deposits into it? It makes no sense."

Kate leaned forward, obviously thinking, as I was, that something wasn't adding up. "Doctor Richardson, have you noticed anything unusual about your other financial accounts or credit reports over the past eighteen months? Any unusual deposits?"

"No, nothing. I monitor my accounts regularly, and I haven't seen any unauthorized activity."

"That's true," Tim said.

"What about your medical practice?" I asked. "Have you been asked to provide consultations or make recommendations that seemed unusual or inappropriate?"

Richardson thought for a moment, then shook her head. "Nothing that stands out. I provide consultations as requested by attending physicians, and I can think of nothing that hasn't been routine and appropriate."

Tim showed her more detailed records, including dates and amounts that corresponded to specific periods when elderly patients under suspicious care had died. "Doctor Richardson, do any of these dates correspond to consultations you provided?" he asked.

She studied the timeline carefully, then nodded and said, "Some of these dates correspond to consultations I provided, but that could be entirely coincidental."

"What kind of consultations?" Kate asked.

"Standard internal medicine reviews. Medication interactions, cardiac function assessments, treatment recommendations for complex geriatric conditions. Nothing unusual or suspicious."

I was becoming more convinced that Richardson was telling the truth, but that raised troubling questions about why someone had been using her identity and how they'd managed to do so without her knowledge.

"Doctor," I said, "if someone has been using your identity to receive payments connected to a murder conspiracy—and it looks like they have—you could be in danger."

She put her hand to her mouth and stared at me. "What do you mean?" she whispered.

"I think you're being set up to take the blame for crimes you didn't commit, and the people behind this conspiracy might view you as a liability that needs to be eliminated."

Her face went pale as the implications sank in. "You think someone is trying to frame me for murder?"

"It's possible," Kate said. "The financial records create a paper trail that suggests your involvement in the conspiracy."

"But why would someone do that?"

"They might need a scapegoat," I replied. "You in your position here in the hospital would, I think, make you the perfect choice."

Richardson was quiet for several minutes, apparently processing the possibility that she'd been manipulated and used without her knowledge. When she spoke again, her voice reflected both fear and determination.

"What can I do to help you find out who these people are?"

"I need you to provide us with complete access to your financial records, medical consultations, and any communications you've had with people connected to this case," Tim said. "Can you do that?"

"Of course," she replied. "I want whoever's been doing this caught and prosecuted."

But Tim was already back to analyzing the financial records, looking for patterns that might reveal who was really controlling the bogus account in Dr.

Richardson's name. "Doctor Richardson," he said after a moment, "do you not have any idea who might have access to your personal information?"

She thought for a moment, shook her head and said, "Hospital personnel records, my bank, my accountant, the medical licensing board. The usual places.."

Kate was making notes as we discussed the possibilities. After a moment, she looked up and said, "I'm afraid we're going to need you to file identity theft reports with your bank and credit agencies."

"I'll do that immediately," Richardson said.

"And we're going to need you to be very careful about your personal security," Kate continued. "One more thing, Doctor, as Mr. Starke already mentioned, if someone has been using your identity for criminal purposes, they might view you as a threat."

Richardson nodded. "Do you really think I'm in danger?"

"We don't know yet," I replied. "It's possible, but until we figure out who's been using your identity and why, you should take precautions."

As we concluded the interview, I couldn't help but believe she was telling the truth. I'd been at this game a long time—so had Kate—and we both knew a liar when we met one. And, if she *was* telling the truth, then someone had been sophisticated enough to use her identity for a year-and-a-half without her knowledge while positioning her as a potential scapegoat for systematic murder. It was mind-blowing, beyond anything I'd ever run into.

"If you'll give us a minute, Doctor," I said, then turned to Kate. "A word?"

Kate nodded and together we stepped out into the corridor, leaving Richardson and Tim still seated at the table.

"Kate," I said, closing the door after Samson slipped through, "if Dr. Richardson is innocent, and I believe she is, then someone has been very clever about covering their tracks."

"And if she's lying, she's one of the best actresses I've ever encountered," Kate replied.

"I think we should check on Maya Santos," Kate said. Then we both turned when we heard someone hurrying along the corridor toward us.

Dr. Walker joined us, looking concerned and slightly out of breath, as if she'd hurried to get there.

19

THE REAL KILLER REVEALED

"I CAME AS SOON AS I HEARD ABOUT WALTER'S DEATH," she said. "This is such a tragedy. How is Maya doing?"

Kate also looked surprised by Dr. Walker's arrival. Samson sat down and stared up at her, his head tilted to one side, his jaws closed tight.

"Doctor Walker, we weren't expecting to see you here today," Kate said. "I'm told Maya's condition is improving, but she's still unconscious."

"I've been so worried about both of them," Walker replied. "Walter was such a sweet man, and Maya seemed so devoted to his care. I can't believe this has happened."

It was at that moment that the conference room door opened and Dr. Richardson stepped out.

"Oh," she said. "I'm sorry. I didn't know…" She stepped forward, extending her hand to Dr. Walker. "I'm Amanda Richardson, internal medicine. We've met before. I've been consulting on Maya Santos's case."

"Oh yes, Doctor Richardson. I remember," Walker replied, sounding somewhat confused, I thought. "I appreciate your involvement in Maya's care."

Something about the interaction between the two doctors caught my attention. There was a formality to their greeting that seemed odd, as if they were meeting for the first time despite both being involved in related cases at the same hospital. The exchange had the quality of a carefully choreographed performance rather than a natural professional interaction.

Tim appeared next, holding one of his laptops in the crook of his arm and with an expression on his face that suggested he'd discovered something important.

"Harry," Tim said urgently, "I've got the results of the financial analysis. I know who it is."

Dr. Richardson looked at him. Her apparent interest in the investigation results seeming genuine but perhaps a bit too intense.

Tim stared at Dr. Walker.

"Tim Clarke, Doctor Walker," I said, introducing them

Tim's eyes opened wide. The doctor smiled at him and held out her hand.

"Tim's my IT specialist," I said. "He's been working the case with me. What did you find, Tim?"

Tim hesitated for a moment, still staring at Dr. Walker, then said, "I know who it is, Harry. I know who we've been looking for."

I noticed Samson's posture change subtly. He stood up, lowered his head, and then looked up at Kate. She noticed it, too.

"Go on," I said.

"It's not Maya," he said. "The evidence points to someone else entirely."

Dr. Walker's expression remained perfectly calm, but I caught a slight tightening around her eyes and I felt the muscles in my gut tighten as I guessed what Tim was about to say next.

"Well, I hope you've found whoever's been responsible for Walter's suffering," Walker said easily.

"Tim," I said, quietly, "what did you find?"

"Look." Tim shifted a little so I could see the screen.

"Who is it?" Kate asked, her hand instinctively moving closer to her weapon as Samson moved in front of her.

Tim looked directly at Dr. Walker. He hesitated, bit his lip, took a deep breath and said, "It's you," he said. "Doctor Patricia Walker."

Walker's reaction was immediate. Her face flushed with indignation, and her voice took on the outraged tone of a respected physician being falsely accused of something heinous.

"That's absolutely ridiculous!" she snapped. "How can you say that? I've dedicated my career to helping elderly patients, including Walter Brennan. How dare you make such accusations!"

"Doctor Walker," Tim continued, consulting his laptop for specific details, "can you explain why you've been receiving monthly payments of twenty-five thousand dollars from the Pinnacle Medical Research Foundation?"

"The foundation pays me for legitimate consulting

services related to geriatric care research," she replied. "There's nothing suspicious about compensation for professional services."

"What about the payments the foundation—which, by the way, is a shell company—has been making to Maya Santos?" Tim asked, and to Doctor Richardson?

Dr. Walker's expression shifted to one of apparent confusion and concern, of someone who was genuinely surprised by disturbing news. "What payments? If Maya has been receiving money from the foundation, it's news to me. Are you suggesting she's been embezzling funds? As to Doctor Richardson; I don't know anything about that either."

"Doctor Walker," Tim said, "the records show that the foundation is registered to you and has been making payments to Maya Santos for over six months."

"That's impossible. I would know about any payments from the foundation. If such payments exist, someone else must have authorized them without my knowledge."

Walker was good—very good. Her denials sounded completely credible, and her suggestion that Maya might be embezzling from the foundation was a clever deflection that played into the existing suspicions about Maya's guilt. The performance was so convincing it almost fooled me.

"We have evidence that you've been coordinating a conspiracy to systematically poison elderly patients and stealing their assets," I said, mildly.

"Mr. Starke, I'm deeply offended by these accusations," Walker snapped. "I've spent fifteen years building a reputation as a caring physician, and I've never done anything to harm any of my patients. If you have concerns about Maya Santos or anyone else, I suggest you investigate them properly instead of making wild accusations against innocent people."

"These records show a pattern of payments and communications that connect you directly to the conspiracy, Doctor Walker."

"Then your records are wrong," she said haughtily. "Either that or someone has been using my identity. I've never participated in any conspiracy, and I resent the implication that I would harm the patients I've devoted my life to helping."

Dr. Richardson looked confused by the exchange, her apparent bewilderment seeming genuine as she tried to understand the accusations being made against a respected colleague. "Doctor Walker," she said, "surely you can provide documentation that can refute these allegations?"

"I can and I will," she snapped, "but I don't appreciate being ambushed with false accusations in a hospital corridor. If you have legitimate concerns about my professional conduct, there are proper channels for addressing them."

Kate was watching Dr. Walker carefully, clearly sensing that something wasn't right about her reactions despite the apparent sincerity of her denials. "Doctor Walker," she said quietly, "we'd like you to come with us to formally review the evidence we've gathered."

"I'm afraid I can't do that right now," she replied,

taking a step back. "I have patients to see and responsibilities to fulfill. If you want to discuss these accusations further, you can contact my attorney."

She started to walk away, but Kate moved to block her path. "We're not finished with this conversation, Doctor Walker," she said.

"Captain Gazzara, unless you're arresting me, I'm free to go about my business. I've answered your questions, and I've explained that your accusations are baseless."

"Actually," I said, "we do have enough evidence to arrest you."

Her demeanor changed in an instant. The professional physician facade dropped away like a discarded mask, and something much more dangerous appeared in her eyes. The transformation was startling. She changed from caring healer to deadly predator in the space of a heartbeat.

"You have no idea what you're dealing with," she snarled.

"We know you've been systematically murdering elderly patients for their money," Tim piped up, his voice squeaky with tension.

"You know nothing." Walker's voice was cold now. All pretense of medical professionalism was gone. "You've stumbled into something far beyond your understanding."

Kate, her hand on her weapon, said, "Doctor Walker, you need to come with us *now!*"

Instead of complying, Dr. Walker reached into her

medical bag and pulled out a huge syringe filled with a clear liquid. The movement was swift and practiced.

"I don't think so," she snarled.

"Drop it!" Kate shouted, drawing her weapon.

But before Kate could draw her weapon, Walker lunged forward, the syringe aimed directly at Kate's neck as she closed the distance between them in two quick steps.

"Kate!" I shouted, but Walker was already on her.

Kate tried to sidestep the attack, but Walker caught her arm, and they grappled for control of the syringe. The two women crashed into the wall, Walker using her leverage to force the needle toward Kate's throat.

"This contains enough concentrated aconitine to kill you within minutes," Walker hissed as they struggled.

Me? I was more than six feet away. I leaped forward, but Samson beat me to it. The big German Shepherd launched himself in one giant leap at Walker. His 115 pounds of muscle hit her squarely in the chest, knocking her backward, sending the syringe flying across the corridor.

Kate staggered backward into me. I grabbed her and stopped her from falling. Walker went down hard with Samson standing over her, his nose only inches from hers, his teeth bared. Looking back on it, I think she was paralyzed by the sight of his huge head so close to her own, but only for a moment, and then she began screaming.

"Get him off me!" Walker screamed, but Samson

didn't move. He held his position until Kate could secure her.

Kate, breathing heavily, stood for a moment, Samson growling deep in the back of his throat, standing over her. Walker tried to move, but Samson snapped his jaws, and she squeaked in terror as drool dripped onto her face.

"Enough, Samson," Kate said, and the big dog immediately backed away, his eyes never leaving Walker's. Kate quickly cuffed her and then hauled her to her feet and stepped away.

"Good boy, Samson," she said, ruffling his ears. "Very good boy."

Tim carefully picked up the syringe, handling it with extreme caution, in respect for the deadly nature of its contents. "Harry, if this really contains aconitine, it's enough to kill a bunch of people."

Dr. Richardson stood frozen against the wall, her face pale with shock at witnessing the violent attack and Dr. Walker's sudden transformation.

I looked at Walker and said, "Now, do you want to tell us the truth?"

All the fight seemed to have gone out of her. Samson's takedown had not only stopped her murder attempt but had also shattered the psychological armor she'd been using to maintain her denials.

"You do not know how carefully this operation was planned," she said, her voice bitter with defeat. "Years of preparation, perfect execution, and you idiots stumbled onto it by accident."

"How many people have you killed?" Kate asked.

"Forty-three over four years. Each one carefully selected, systematically eliminated, and properly processed. It was a perfect system until that paranoid old man's daughter had to hire you."

"Doctor Walker, you're under arrest for the murder of Helen Foster, James Morrison, and Walter Brennan—"

"Walter Brennan," she snapped, interrupting her. "He was supposed to be the crown jewel of the operation," she continued. "Eighty million dollars that would have funded my research for decades. But his paranoid daughter had to interfere, and Maya had to develop a conscience."

"So you decided to eliminate them both," I said.

"Maya was always expendable. Helen Foster and James Morrison became problems when they started interfering. Their elimination was necessary."

I couldn't believe what I was hearing, and how coldly she was telling it.

I looked at Tim. He was recording everything on his laptop.

"How did you select your victims?" I asked.

"We chose wealthy, isolated elderly people with minimal family oversight. They were suffering anyway. I simply managed their transitions while ensuring their assets were used for meaningful research purposes."

Dr. Richardson finally found her voice. "Patricia, how could you? We took an oath to do no harm."

"I did no harm," Walker replied coldly. "I provided

services that advanced medical knowledge while helping people who were dying anyway to die... peacefully and painlessly."

As two of Kate's officer prepared to take Walker away, she looked at us with cold calculation.

"You think you've won something here, but you have no idea how many people are involved in this operation. This is bigger than your small-town investigation."

"We'll find them, don't you worry," Kate said.

"Will you?" She smiled skeptically. "Some of them are people you trust, people in positions of authority. You've stopped just one small part of a much larger business."

As the elevator doors closed on Dr. Walker and the arresting officers, the hospital corridor fell quiet.

"Kate," I said, "Samson saved your life."

Kate knelt down to praise the German Shepherd, who was panting slowly. "Good boy, Samson," she whispered in his ear. "You're a hero, again."

Richardson looking shaken. "I can't believe she was capable of something like this," she muttered, almost to herself. She looked at me and said, "And I was being set up to take the blame."

"Yes, you were," said. I would have said more, but what was the point? There was nothing I could say that would have made her feel any better about it. So I said no more.

Tim closed his laptop and looked at us. "So what now?" he asked. "She mentioned there was an entire network of people."

"Now we unravel the rest of it," Kate said. "But first, we need to check on Maya and make sure she's okay. If what Walker said is true, she could still be a target. We give them time to get her booked in, then we'll go and with her. We have the evidence we need, but a confession on the record would be nice."

20

FULL CONFESSION

THE INTERROGATION ROOM AT POLICE HEADQUARTERS felt different than usual as Kate prepared to question Dr. Patricia Walker. I was invited to sit in on it with Kate. This wasn't a routine criminal interview. We were about to confront someone who had confessed to systematically murdered dozens of people. The weight of forty-three lives hung in the air as we reviewed our strategy one last time, knowing that this confession could be crucial to securing justice for the victims.

The room itself seemed to reflect the gravity of what we were about to undertake. The fluorescent lights cast harsh shadows across the metal table, the recording equipment hummed quietly in the background, and the red lights on the two cameras glowed steadily, ready to capture every word of what we hoped would be a comprehensive admission of guilt. The institutional green walls had witnessed countless confessions over the years, but none involving crimes of this magnitude and sophistication.

Dr. Walker sat across from us with her attorney, a sharp-looking woman named Margaret Court—kind of appropriate, I thought—who specialized in defending medical professionals accused of malpractice and criminal conduct. Despite the handcuffs and orange jumpsuit, Walker maintained an air of professional composure, as if this were simply another challenging medical consultation rather than an interrogation about serial murder.

"Doctor Walker," Kate began, "you're here because you've already admitted to killing Walter Brennan, Helen Foster, and James Morrison. I must now caution you that you have the right to remain silent…"

I watched Walker as Kate continued to read her her rights. She remained stoic throughout.

"You have already admitted that you murdered—"

"My client has not admitted to anything," Attorney Court interrupted her sharply. "Doctor Walker was under extreme duress when those statements were made, and anything she said at the hospital should be considered inadmissible."

Kate leaned forward, her expression serious. Me? I couldn't help but smile. This wasn't Kate's first rodeo, as they say. She had more than twenty years of experience interrogating dangerous criminals to draw on, so she simply continued without even looking at the attorney; it was the ultimate putdown. "As I was saying, Doctor Walker, you have already admitted to forty-one murders, including those of Walter Brennan, Hellen Foster, and James Morrison, and we have substantial evidence connecting you to a conspiracy that spans five states. Your cooperation now could make a significant difference in how this case is prosecuted."

Court said nothing. Walker studied Kate's face for a long moment, then she looked at me with the calculating gaze of someone who'd spent years manipulating people and situations to her advantage. There was something unsettling about her clinical assessment of our demeanor and motivations, as if she were still trying to diagnose and treat a medical condition rather than facing the consequences of systematic murder.

"What exactly do you want to know?" she asked, ignoring her attorney's sharp look of disapproval.

"Why don't you begin at the beginning," Kate said. "How the operation works, who's involved, how you selected your victims, and how you managed to avoid detection for so long."

Walker was quiet for several minutes, apparently weighing her options, probably with the same methodical approach she'd used when planning her victims' deaths. When she finally spoke, her voice carried the tone of someone who'd decided that cooperation might be her best chance of avoiding the death penalty.

"It started almost accidentally," she said, her voice taking on the matter-of-fact tone of someone recounting a medical case study. "About five years ago, I had an elderly patient named Dorothy McCann who was suffering from severe depression and social isolation after her husband died. She had substantial assets but no close family, and she was essentially waiting to die. Indeed, she told me she was."

"What happened to her?" Kate asked.

"Dorothy developed complications from her medications; interactions that caused cardiac arrhythmias. When she died, she left a substantial bequest to my research foundation because I'd been one of the few people who'd shown her genuine care and attention during her final months."

Court was taking notes while clearly disapproving of her client's decision to provide detailed information about potentially criminal activities.

"That gave me the idea for a more systematic approach to helping elderly people who were suffering from isolation and neglect while ensuring their assets were used for meaningful purposes rather than being wasted by ungrateful families."

"So you decided to start killing patients for their money," Kate said.

She nodded. "I decided to provide end-of-life services that addressed the real needs of elderly people while creating sustainable funding for research that could help thousands of others in similar situations."

Walker's ability to reframe systematic murder as compassionate medical care was both fascinating and disturbing. She'd clearly spent years developing justifications that allowed her to maintain her self-image as a caring physician even while committing heinous crimes against the people who trusted her most.

"How did you select your victims?" I asked.

She looked at me, smiled, and said, "Clients," Mr. Starke, "not victims. I selected my clients based on specific criteria that ensured the services I provided would be both needed and effective."

"Criteria?" I said, wondering how this creature could live with herself. "What criteria?"

"Substantial assets, minimal family oversight, existing health conditions that provided cover for medical intervention, and social isolation that prevented interference with their care."

"Huh!" Kate said. I glanced at her. Her face was pale. "How did you identify people who met these criteria?"

"Through my medical practice, professional networks, and referrals from other healthcare providers. Elderly people who fit the profile often came to my attention through routine medical consultations or referrals from colleagues who were dealing with difficult cases."

"What about Maya Santos?" I asked. "How did she become involved?"

Walker's expression shifted slightly, and I wondered if Maya's involvement had been more complex than the simple employee relationship she'd initially described.

"Maya was recruited through a placement agency that specializes in providing caregivers for high-net-worth elderly clients. She had financial pressures that made her willing to accept employment arrangements that included... additional responsibilities."

"Such as?" Kate asked, her eyes narrowed, her brow wrinkled.

"Providing detailed reports about the clients' daily activities," she replied calmly, "family relationships, and financial affairs. Administering supplements and medications as directed. Facilitating social isolation by discouraging contact with family members who might interfere with their care."

"And poisoning them," I said.

"Maya knew nothing. She couldn't be trusted. She administered nothing she knew was harmful. She was told the supplements and medications were part of specialized treatment protocols designed to improve the clients' quality of life."

Court leaned forward, her professional concern for her client overriding her disapproval of the confession. "Doctor Walker, I strongly advise you to stop providing details about alleged criminal activities."

"Margaret, they already have enough evidence to convict me of multiple murders. Cooperation is might be my only chance of avoiding execution."

"Doctor Walker," I said, "what exactly did Maya think she was doing?"

"Maya believed she was providing enhanced medical care under my supervision. She was told that the elderly clients required specialized treatments that weren't available through standard healthcare channels."

"Did she know the clients were dying because of the treatments?"

"Maya knew the clients were declining and eventually dying, but she was told it was because of the natural progression of their medical conditions. She was led to believe that the treatments were extending their lives and improving their comfort, not causing their deaths."

"How did you manage to avoid detection by other medical professionals?" Kate asked.

"By working within the existing healthcare system rather than outside it. The clients received legitimate medical care from multiple providers, and the substances I administered were designed to interact with their prescribed medications in ways that mimicked natural disease progression."

"What kind of substances?" I asked.

"Primarily plant-based alkaloids that cause cardiac and neurological symptoms consistent with age-related decline," she replied. "Aconitine from monks-hood plants, digitalis compounds from foxglove, and various other naturally occurring toxins that are diffi-cult to detect in standard medical examinations."

"And how did you obtain these substances?" Kate asked.

"Some I extracted from plants I cultivated myself," she replied. "Others were obtained through contacts in the pharmaceutical research community who believed I was conducting legitimate studies on the therapeutic properties of natural compounds."

Dr. Walker's description of her methods revealed a level of sophistication that made my head spin. She'd essentially weaponized legitimate medical knowledge.

Kate nodded. "Who are the other people involved in your… operation?"

Walker didn't hesitate. "Thomas McKinnon handled legal aspects: estate planning, will modifications, probate proceedings, etcetera. He understood the clients were being helped to transition out of life, and he ensured that the legal processes were handled efficiently."

"Did he know you were murdering people?" Kate asked.

She smiled. "Thomas knew the clients were receiving specialized end-of-life care that shortened their suffering while ensuring their assets were properly managed. He may have suspected the specific methods, but he never asked for details."

"What about Patricia Stevens?" I asked. By now, I was totally hooked by the saga that was playing out in that cheerless room.

"Patricia managed logistics: identifying potential clients, coordinating caregiver placements, handling financial transfers. She was essential to the operation's success."

"And she knew about the murders?" Kate asked, after glancing at me.

"Patricia knew that the operation involved helping elderly clients transition peacefully while preserving their assets for charitable purposes," Walker replied. "The specific medical aspects were my responsibility."

Kate leaned back in her chair, her expression blank. I could tell she was stunned by what she was hearing, as was I. We were watching, and listening to, a cold-hearted monster justifying her actions, if only to herself.

"Doctor Walker," Kate said, obviously dumbfounded. "What you're describing is a conspiracy to systematically commit elder abuse and murder on a grand scale."

"What I'm describing," she declared, "is a business model that provided needed services while generating sustainable funding for important medical research. That some participants may not have understood all aspects of the operation doesn't change the fundamental purpose."

"Which was to steal money from elderly people by killing them," I said, also dumbfounded by both her narrative and demeanor.

"Which was to provide comprehensive end-of-life services that addressed real medical and social needs while ensuring that substantial assets were used for meaningful purposes," she insisted.

I was struck by Walker's absolute commitment to her twisted justifications. Even facing life in prison or execution, she continued to present what she'd done as compassionate medical care. Her ability to maintain these delusions was both remarkable and, at the same time, terrifying.

"How many healthcare providers were involved in your operation?" Kate asked, her eyes closed.

"Several physicians provided prescriptions and medical consultations without being aware of the full scope of the treatment protocols. They believed they were providing legitimate medical care for elderly patients with complex conditions."

"Such as Doctor Richardson?"

"Amanda Richardson? I didn't know her well, but she was one of several physicians who provided medical services as requested. She may have suspected that her prescriptions were being used in conjunction with other treatments, but she never asked for specific details."

"How many unwitting accomplices were there?" I asked.

She shrugged. "Dozens of healthcare providers, attorneys, financial advisors, and other professionals provided services that supported the operation. Most of them believed they were taking part in legitimate medical and legal activities."

Court was shaking her head at her client's continued revelations, her professional training warring with her obvious desire to protect her client from further self-incrimination. "Doctor Walker," she said, "you're implicating numerous people in criminal activities."

"I'm explaining how a sophisticated medical opera-tion required the cooperation of multiple profession-als," she stated, "most of whom were unaware of the broader context of their contributions."

Kate shook her head, took a moment, then said, "Very well, we've established your motives. Let's move on. Let's talk about Walter Brennan. Why did you target him?"

"Walter represented the ideal client," she replied. "Substantial assets, strained family relationships, existing health conditions, and social isolation. His case also represented an opportunity to establish a substantial endowment that could fund my research for decades."

"How long had you been planning his murder?" Kate asked.

"Walter's care plan was developed over approximately six months. The systematic approach required careful preparation to ensure that his decline appeared natural and that his family's concerns could be dismissed as normal eldercare conflicts."

"And Maya's role?" I asked.

"Maya was positioned to provide daily access to Walter while documenting his declining condition and facilitating his isolation from family members who might try to interfere with his care."

"Did Maya know she was helping you kill Walter?" Kate asked.

"As I've already stated, Maya believed she was providing enhanced medical support under my supervision. She was told that Walter's supplements and medications were part of a specialized treatment protocol designed to improve his cognitive function and physical health."

"But instead, they were slowly poisoning him," I said, then took a very deep breath.

"They were carefully calibrated to interact with his prescribed medications in ways that would cause gradual decline consistent with natural aging processes," she insisted.

I leaned forward, focusing on the specific murders that had drawn us into this case. "What about Helen Foster and James Morrison?" I asked. "Why did you kill them?"

"Helen Foster was conducting an unauthorized investigation into Walter's care that threatened to expose the treatment protocol before it could be completed," she said coldly. "Her elimination became necessary when she began documenting information that could compromise the operation."

"And Morrison?" I asked.

"James was cooperating with Helen's investigation and he'd begun keeping detailed records of activities around the Brennan household. His continued surveillance posed an unacceptable risk to the operation's security."

"So you murdered them to cover up your crimes," I said, wearily.

"I simply eliminated threats to Walter's care plan that could have prevented him from receiving the proper comprehensive treatment he needed."

Kate shook her head at Dr. Walker's continued use of euphemisms to describe cold-blooded murder. "But you were *killing them,*" she snapped.

Walker didn't answer. She simply took a deep breath and sat up straighter, her head tilted slightly to the right, and looked defiantly at Kate.

"How did you kill Helen Foster?" I asked, resignedly.

"Helen received an injection of concentrated digitalis that caused cardiac arrest consistent with her existing heart condition. The timing and method were designed to appear as death from natural causes."

"And Morrison?" I asked.

"James was eliminated through exposure to phosphine gas in a confined space. The method was chosen to appear as an accidental death involving the pesticide equipment he used regularly."

"You sabotaged the ventilation system in the greenhouse?"

"I modified the safety systems to ensure that the gas would accumulate to effective levels while appearing to be an equipment malfunction."

"What about Helen Foster specifically? How did you get access to her?" I asked, thinking that, at that moment, Kate was essentially done, perplexed, confounded, floored by what she heard, by what she was hearing. She was sitting back in her chair with her arms folded across her chest, staring at the doctor.

Dr. Walker showed a flicker of what might have been regret, but I doubt it. "Helen was the most dangerous threat to the operation. Her investigation was systematic and professional. She was documenting everything and getting too close to exposing the entire network."

"But how did you get to her?" I asked.

"I made routine house calls to check on Walter's condition. As his primary physician, I had legitimate access to the property at any time. Helen never suspected that the doctor she trusted was actually responsible for Walter's systematic poisoning."

There it was, the first time she'd used the word 'poisoning.'

"I arrived to check on Walter's medication adjustments," Walker continued, "and Helen was in the kitchen preparing his evening meal. She'd been asking too many questions about Walter's symptoms and Maya's care protocols."

"So you killed her during your house call," I stated.

"I told Helen I needed to discuss Walter's dietary restrictions with her privately," she said. "While we were talking in the kitchen, I administered an injection of concentrated digitalis that caused immediate cardiac arrest. The injection site was so small I thought it would be missed during standard autopsy procedures."

"While Maya was upstairs with Walter?" I asked, trying to establish Maya's innocence.

"Yes. Maya was occupied with Walter's afternoon care routine. She had no idea what I was doing in the kitchen."

"Helen trusted you as Walter's physician," Hate said, quietly.

"Helen's trust in medical authority made her elimination possible. She never suspected that the doctor she was confiding her concerns to was actually the person orchestrating Walter's systematic murder."

I blew out a breath, shook my head and said, "Geez, you really are something, aren't you, Doctor?"

She looked a little uncomfortable, but she didn't answer.

Court looked like she wanted to physically restrain her client from providing additional incriminating details. "Doctor Walker," she whispered, "please consider the implications of these statements."

Walker shook her head, but didn't reply. Court sat back in her seat and folded her arm, essentially washing her hands of what had already turned into a losing situation.

"Doctor Walker," I said, "what was your plan for Maya Santos?"

"Maya's elimination was always part of the operational timeline," she replied coldly. "Once Walter's care was completed and the estate transfers were finalized, Maya would be eliminated through apparent suicide, leaving behind a note regretting her guilt over her participation in elder abuse."

"But Walter and Maya both survived your final murder attempts," I said.

"Walter proved more resilient than I expected," she replied, "and Maya survived an overdose that should have been fatal. I'm not quite sure what happened there, unfortunate though it was."

Again, I couldn't help but shake my head.

Kate uncrossed her arms, sat up straight, and said, "I've had enough of this. Doctor Walker, you've confessed to murdering forty-three elderly people over four years. Do you understand the implications and magnitude of what you've done?"

"I think so," she replied. "I've provided end-of-life services to forty-three clients who were suffering from isolation, neglect, and declining health while ensuring that their assets were used for research that could help thousands of others in similar situations."

"You've committed serial murder for financial gain," Kate snapped.

"I've practiced medicine in a way that addresses real problems in our society while creating sustainable funding for important research."

Even in the face of overwhelming evidence and certain conviction, Dr. Walker maintained her delusion that systematic murder had been compassionate medical care. Her ability to rationalize and justify her crimes was both remarkable and terrifying.

"Doctor Walker," I said, "is there anything else you want to tell us about your operation and the people who were involved?"

"The work I was doing was important and necessary. Elderly people in our society suffer from abandonment, isolation, and inadequate medical care while their assets are wasted by families who don't appreciate them. I provided a solution that addressed real needs while creating meaningful benefits for society."

"You really believe that, don't you?" I said. "But did you ever discuss what you were doing with your victims? Surely life is precious even to the terminally ill?"

"With respect, Mr. Starke, you have not seen the level of suffering I have seen," she replied. "By providing comprehensive services that helped the suffering transition peacefully and painlessly, while ensuring their resources were used for purposes that would help others."

As the interrogation concluded, I was struck by Dr. Walker's absolute refusal to acknowledge the criminal and immoral nature of her actions. She'd constructed such a compendium of elaborate justifications for what she was doing that she genuinely believed she'd been providing valuable medical services rather than committing heinous crimes.

"Doctor Walker," Kate said as we prepared to end the session, "I'm charging you with the first-degree murders of Walter Brennan, Helen Foster, and James

Morrison. You will also be charged with a further forty-one counts of first-degree murder, multiple counts of conspiracy to commit murder, fraud, and numerous other charges related to your criminal operation."

"I understand that you have to prosecute me according to the law, but I hope that someday society will recognize the value of the work I was doing and the importance of the research it funded."

"The only thing society will recognize is that you're a serial killer who exploited the trust placed in medical professionals to commit systematic murder for personal gain," Kate snapped, as she stood up and turned to the officer standing at the back of the room. "Take her away."

21

JUSTICE AND RESOLUTION

THREE MONTHS AFTER DR. PATRICIA WALKER'S ARREST, the Chattanooga courthouse was packed with family members of her victims, reporters, and law enforcement officials. The "Doctor Death" case had become one of the largest elder abuse prosecutions in modern American legal history.

I sat in the gallery with Amanda, watching Judge Rhonda Chesterton prepare to deliver sentences. Kate sat two rows ahead with Samson at her feet, the German Shepherd wearing his official badge and harness.

Dr. Walker sat at the defendant's table in an orange jumpsuit, looking smaller and more ordinary than someone who had orchestrated the enormity of crimes she had. The months in jail had clearly taken their toll.

"Patricia Walker," Judge Morrison began, "you have been found guilty on forty-three counts of first-degree murder, conspiracy to murder, identity fraud, and elder abuse. Do you have anything to say before I impose sentence?"

Dr. Walker stood slowly. "Your Honor, I deeply regret the pain my actions have caused. What I thought was compassionate medical care was actually an abomination, and I take full responsibility for my actions."

It was the first time she had acknowledged her actions as criminal rather than medical. Several family members wiped away tears as they heard their loved ones' killer finally admit to her crimes.

"I know nothing I say can bring back the people whose life I took," she continued. "I can only hope my cooperation with law enforcement has helped bring justice and prevented others from suffering the same fate. I have nothing more to say, your honor." And she sat down.

Judge Chesterton reviewed the extensive documentation. "In my thirty years on the bench, I have never encountered such systematic, calculated criminal activity. You used your position as a trusted medical professional to exploit vulnerable elderly people who depended on you for care. You murdered forty-three innocent people as part of a business operation designed to steal their money. The betrayal of trust is almost beyond comprehension."

The judge paused. "The court acknowledges your cooperation and apparent acceptance of responsibility. However, the magnitude of your crimes demands the most severe punishment I can impose. On each of the forty-three counts of first-degree murder, I sentence you to life in prison without the possibility of parole.

These sentences are to run consecutively. You will also make restitution of $47.3 million to the families of your victims."

There was more, of course, a long litany that seemed to go on forever, as would Dr' Walker's life behind bars. As she was led away in shackles, family members in the gallery clapped; justice had finally been served.

Twenty minutes later, out on the courthouse steps, reporters crowded around us.

"Captain Gazzara, what's the status of the other network members?" one called out.

"Thomas McKinnon received twenty-five years in federal prison," Kate replied. "Patricia Stevens got fifteen years. Several others are still being prosecuted in various jurisdictions."

"What about Maya Santos?" Another called out.

"Maya has been cleared of all charges," Kate replied. "The evidence showed she was manipulated and exploited by Dr. Walker. Maya was as much a victim as the elderly people who were murdered. She believed she was providing enhanced medical care and had no knowledge the treatments were actually poison."

As we drove away, Amanda asked, "How is Maya really doing?"

"I'm not sure," I replied, as I turned onto Scenic Highway, heading home. "Better than expected, I think. The counseling is helping her understand she was manipulated, not complicit, but she has a long way to go. She was devastated by what happened to her... and

Walter, and I have to wonder if she'll ever really get over it."

"What about the Brennan family?" Amanda asked.

At that, I smiled. It was kind of ironic... "Walter never signed the new will, so Lisa and Mark inherited as originally intended. Now they're saying they wish they'd been more involved in his care."

My phone rang. It was Kate. I tapped the Blue Tooth and took the call. "Harry, the feds authorities have arrested eleven other physicians across six states, including Tennessee, and the hunt goes on. I thought you'd like to know."

"Thanks, Kate. We're on our way home. Keep me posted, will you?"

"Any word on Ruth Webb?" Amanda asked as I made the turn at the top of the mountain onto East Brow Road.

"Ruth's working with FBI. She's considering becoming a licensed private investigator."

That evening, after we'd put Jade to bed, as Amanda and I sat on the wall overlooking the city below, contemplating the lessons of the past week, I reflected on the importance of listening to elderly people when they express concerns, even when their complaints seem paranoid.

"So what's next, Harry?" Amanda asked.

I shrugged. "More of the same, I suppose. Cases that matter, people who need help."

"No more serial killers, I hope," she muttered with a smile as she lifted her drink to her lips.

I laughed. "Me, too," I said. "But you never know

where a case will lead. What looks like a simple problem can often turn out to be something much bigger."

It was a beautiful evening. The moon was up, the city below was a field of twinkling lights, and great was a riband of glittering silver meandering through city toward the lights of the Sequoya nuclear plant on the horizon to the east.

I reached out and took Amanda's hand in mine. "Hey," I said. "It's a wonderful life we have, you know."

She shifted closer to me, leaned her head on my shoulder, sighed and said, "I know."

It was enough. I lifted my glass of Laphroaig to my lips and took a sip, savoring the taste as it slid smoothly down my throat, the magnificent view, and my beautiful fife at my side.

Life was good.

22

FINAL JUDGMENT

Six months after Dr. Walker's sentencing, I returned to Walter Brennan's former estate. Lisa and Mark had decided to sell the property and donate the proceeds to a foundation dedicated to preventing elder abuse.

The estate looked different in the autumn light, somehow smaller and less imposing. The gardens Jim Morrison had tended showed signs of neglect, and the greenhouse where he'd died remained locked.

I was meeting Kate and Tim. It was an informal tradition we'd begun some twelve months earlier, to revisit the scene of a significant case to reflect on what was and what might have been. It wasn't something I would normally have gone for, but it was Tim's idea, and, well, *why the hell not,* I thought. Kate arrived with Samson a few minutes after I did. She turned the big dog loose and he who immediately began exploring the grounds, giving the flowerbeds close attention. A minute later he was off after a squirrel, which he had no chance of catching, but it was fun to watch him try.

"Hard to believe it all started here," Kate said, watching Samson trotting round the greenhouse.

"With Lisa Brennan in my office, worried about her father's caregiver," I replied. "If I hadn't trusted her instincts, Dr. Walker might still be killing elderly people."

Tim joined us, his hands in his jeans pockets, the ever-present iPad under his left arm. "The final count is sixty-seven victims across eight states over six years," he said. "Forty-three that the good doctor murdered, and twenty-four more by physicians and caregivers in her network."

"Sixty-seven," Kate repeated. "And we almost missed it entirely."

Even with Walker in prison, it was still hard to believe. "If Walter hadn't saved samples of his food and medication," I said. "If Maya hadn't survived, if Ruth hadn't continued Helen's investigation... Geez, she would have gotten away with it, you know?"

No one answered. I think they were a bumfuzzled as I was. "What's the status of McKinnon and Stevens?" I asked.

"McKinnon is serving his twenty-five years, federal," Tim replied. "Stevens got fifteen and is cooperating."

"Dr. Richardson received five years for her unwitting participation and she lost her medical license," Kate said. "Can you believe it?"

"That's a bit harsh, isn't it?" I said.

"The consensus was that, as an MD, she should have paid more attention and, if she had, she would have picked up on what Walker was doing. There's something to that, I think.

Have you heard anything about Maya?" I asked.

"She doing much better," Kate replied. "She's completed counseling and has started work with elder abuse prevention NGO. No charges were laid against her and she received a settlement from Dr. Walker's assets, so she was good."

We walked together toward the main house, where Walter had spent his last months, convinced he was being poisoned. His instincts were correct. Unfortunately, he didn't survive Walker's final visit.

"The hardest part," I said, "is knowing how many times Walter tried to tell people what was happening, and how many times he was ignored."

"By his children, by law enforcement, by medical professionals," Kate added. "Everyone except Helen Foster and James Morrison."

We stood in the library where Walter had shown us his labeled collection of evidence, samples dismissed as paranoid behavior that ultimately provided crucial evidence for the prosecution.

"This case changed how I think about elder abuse," Kate said. "Doctor Walker's operation shows how medical professionals can exploit the elderly, but there's not much can be done about it, is there?"

I sighed and shook my head. "No, not much... It's the betrayal of trust that makes it so heinous."

"I hear Ruth Webb got her private investigator license," Tim said. "And that she's opening her own agency in Nashville, specializing in elder abuse investigations."

"Helen Foster would be proud," Kate said. "You know, this case has made me think differently about every elder abuse call we get," she continued. "Never again am I going to assume an elderly person's fears are paranoia."

"That might be the most important lesson we've learned," I replied. "Walter's complaints seemed unrealistic because we couldn't imagine how a respected physician could systematically poison patients for money."

When I arrived home, Jade was waiting with questions.

"Did you learn anything new?" Amanda asked.

"Mostly confirmation of what we already knew," I said, not really wanting to talk about it.

Amanda got the message, but Jade didn't. She looked up from homework and said, "Daddy, are there other bad doctors like Dr. Walker?"

"I'm sure there are, sweetheart. But there are also many more good doctors than there are bad ones, so there's nothing for you to worry about, okay?"

"Okay, if you say so," she replied, looking down at the picture she was coloring.

I went to the window and looked out. Chattanooga was settling into another peaceful evening. But I knew that out there somewhere, some elderly person was being mistreated by their caregiver and I couldn't get my head around it. "Why would they do that?" I muttered. "How could they do that?"

"What was that, Harry?" Amanda asked from the doorway.

"Nothing, sweetheart," I said. "Just talking to myself... Just... talking... to myself."

THANK YOU FOR READING, The Inheritance, Book 25 of the Harry Starke Novels. I hope you have enjoyed it and will let others know about my series. I have a full list of my books on the next page.

Have you read my short novella, Buried Secrets yet? It's a prequel to Harrys story. It's available at my store, and at most retailers.

From Blair Howard

The Harry Starke Genesis Series
9 Books in Series as of 2025

The Harry Starke Series
25 Books in Series as of 2025

The Lt. Kate Gazzara Murder Files
21 Books in Series as of 2025

Randall And Carver Mysteries
4 Books in Series as of 2025

The Peacemaker Series
3 Books in Series as of 2025

The O'Sullivan Chronicles: Civil War Series
5 Books in Series as of 2025

From Blair C. Howard

The Sovereign Star Series
7 Books in Series as of 2025

Also available in German

The Predecessor Series
1 Book in Series as of 2025

ABOUT THE AUTHOR

Blair Howard is a retired journalist turned novelist. He's the author of more than 50 novels including the international best-selling Harry Starke series of detective crime stories, the Lt. Kate Gazzara Police Procedural series, the Harry Starke Genesis series, and the Randall & Carver Mysteries. He's also the author of the Peacemaker series of international spy thrillers and five Civil War/Western novels.

If you enjoy reading Science Fiction thrillers, Mr. Howard has made his debut into the genre with, The Sovereign Stars Series under the name, Blair C. Howard.

www.BlairHowardBooks.com